Readers love
STEPHEN OSBORNE

The Scarlet Tide

"A fun, sarcastic, interesting and quirky detective series that I thoroughly enjoy."

—Gay List Book Reviews

"I'm glad to see that Nick plays a more prominent role and hope to see more of him in the next book. Maybe Mr. Osborne can come up with a way the three guys can be happy together…that would make me happy."

—Literary Nymphs

"I both can't wait for and am scared of the next installment. This series certainly isn't your normal m/m romance."

—Live your Life, Buy the Book

Pale as a Ghost

"This book was funny, bloody, suspenseful, and a really good love story. The love story is left open for future books which I didn't mind because I can't imagine it being tied up neatly."

—Live your Life, Buy the Book

By STEPHEN OSBORNE

Cuddling (Dreamspinner Anthology)
Pop Goes the Weasel • Rat Bastard
Temporal Driftwood
Wrestling with Jesus

DUNCAN ANDREWS THRILLERS
Pale as a Ghost
Animal Instinct
The Scarlet Tide
Dead End

Published by DREAMSPINNER PRESS
http://www.dreamspinnerpress.com

DEAD END

END

STEPHEN OSBORNE

Dreamspinner Press

Published by
DREAMSPINNER PRESS

5032 Capital Circle SW, Suite 2, PMB# 279, Tallahassee, FL 32305-7886 USA
http://www.dreamspinnerpress.com/

Dead End
© 2014 Stephen Osborne.

Cover Art
© 2014 Anne Cain.
annecain.art@gmail.com
Cover content is for illustrative purposes only and any person depicted on the cover is a model.

ISBN: 978-1-63216-027-0
Digital ISBN: 978-1-63216-028-7
Library of Congress Control Number: 2014943204
First Edition August 2014

Printed in the United States of America
∞
This paper meets the requirements of
ANSI/NISO Z39.48-1992 (Permanence of Paper).

For John Inman.

CHAPTER 1

THERE HAD been a face in the mirror. A face that shouldn't have been there. A face of pure, primal evil.

Jason Church stood still, staring at the tarnished surface of the hall mirror, trying to convince himself it had been an illusion, some distortion caused by defects in the backing or the mirror's surface. That, of course, was the logical explanation, coupled with an active imagination. He knew, though, that the face had been there. Glaring at him for just a second. Welcoming him to the house. Letting him know the terrors of his childhood would come back with a vengeance.

"Are you just going to stand there? We've still got a lot of stuff to haul in, and I'd like to get all the boxes in by dinnertime."

The sound of Anthony's voice broke Jason out of his trance. He took one last look in the mirror to assure himself the face wasn't there. There was just his reflection, that of a man in his early thirties with a bit of a receding hairline and a goatee. No face with sneering lips and eyes blazing with hatred.

Jason sighed and turned, shifting the box in his arms so he had a better grip on it. Coming up the stairs was his lover, Anthony. He was toting two boxes, one on top of the other. "Probably not the best thing, carrying two boxes up the stairs. You'll fall and break your neck."

"They're not heavy" was Anthony's reply. The top box was obscuring the bottom of his face, but Jason knew his boyfriend was grinning. Anthony was a fitness trainer and liked to show off how strong he was. Even when it wasn't the most prudent thing to do.

"We're not in that much of a hurry. The house is ours. We have all the time in the world." Despite himself, Jason glanced at the mirror again. Just himself and Anthony. The creepy feeling he'd had, the one that seemed to make the hairs on the back of his neck bristle, was gone as well. Just a normal mirror in a normal hallway, in a normal house. It had just been his imagination.

"Where do we want these?" Anthony's voice showed just a hint of strain, making Jason wonder if Anthony's assurance that the boxes weren't heavy was true.

"Middle bedroom. I figured since we wouldn't be using that room for a while, we could use it as a sort of storage until we figure out where we want everything."

"Why this room?" Anthony was already crossing the threshold, clearly aching to put the boxes down as soon as possible.

"Because it's in the worst condition. Wallpaper's peeling, and the ceiling has a huge crack in it. I figured it would take us a couple of weeks before we even thought about tackling it. Plus, when Gary gets here, I'm sure he'll want the bedroom at the opposite end of the hall from us. Besides, it has better closet space for all his junk."

Gary was supposed to have helped out with the moving, but the fourteen-year-old was still with his grandmother, who, it seemed, suddenly needed Gary to stay an extra day to help with yard work. Jason suspected Anthony's son had concocted the "yard work" scheme just to get out of helping with the move. Not that Jason blamed the kid. If he could have come up with an excuse, Jason would have avoided lugging boxes and furniture in from the cold as well.

"Good idea." Anthony let out an involuntary grunt as he placed the boxes in the center of the room. He straightened and glanced back, as if challenging Jason to make a comment.

Jason hesitated, forcing himself not to glance once more at the mirror. Had that mirror been there when he'd been a kid, visiting his aunt's house? He couldn't recall. During those few visits to Aunt Jane's, Jason had avoided going upstairs. He hadn't liked the feel of that part of the house. Perhaps it had been the old staircase, with the creaking steps and the balustrade in need of repair. It had seemed like something out of *Scooby-Doo,* and young Jason had been sure there were vampires and werewolves lurking in the shadows at the top of the stairs.

"Just going to stand there in the hall?" Anthony asked.

"Coming." Jason moved forward but didn't get far. One step into the bedroom, and he stopped as if he'd hit a brick wall. His arms went limp, and the box he was carrying tumbled to the floor. Something inside shattered, but the sound barely registered in Jason's ears. Suddenly, his vision was dimming, and he found it hard to breathe. Part of him was cognizant of dropping the box and the worried look on Anthony's face, but these things seemed far off and disconnected from himself. He bent forward, hoping to get some blood flow to his brain. He felt nauseous and—impossibly—it seemed like the floor was attempting to swallow him up. Like the very room was going to devour him, make him part of the house.

"Are you okay?"

Jason knew Anthony was speaking to him, yet he was frozen and incapable of speech. His mind didn't seem to be working properly. The synapses just weren't firing. He saw Anthony coming over to him, but his boyfriend's movement had a dreamlike quality, unreal but real. He barely felt Anthony's arms on him, helping him up and back out into the hall.

And then the feeling passed. As soon as he was out of the room, the spell was broken. Jason took a deep breath as his head cleared. "Sorry," he said. "Felt faint for a minute there."

"Maybe we've been overdoing it. Let's go downstairs, and I'll make us some coffee. We'll take a little break."

Jason nodded weakly. "Coffee sounds good."

Coffee ended up being more of a chore than either expected, as the coffeemaker was still packed away, so they settled for beer. Jason sat at the kitchen table, feeling like a limp rag, barely looking up when Anthony set the longneck in front of him. "Thanks."

Anthony opened his bottle with one swift twist and settled back against the counter by the sink. As he drank, he didn't take his eyes off

Jason. He was nearly through with his beer before Jason, with slightly shaky hands, even opened his.

"You sure you're okay?" Anthony asked.

"I'm fine." Jason took a small sip and then just held the bottle. He liked the feel of the cold glass in his hands.

"What happened up there?"

Jason didn't answer right away. He sipped again, then set the bottle in front of him. "I'm not sure, to tell you the truth."

"Should we take you to a doctor?"

"Maybe a witch doctor," Jason replied with a mirthless chuckle. "Or maybe we should just call Ghostbusters."

"Say what?" There was still concern in Anthony's voice, but it was now tinged with a little skepticism, as if he was wondering if Jason was putting him on.

"Remember how I told you that, as a child, I always thought this house was haunted?" Jason twisted his neck, working out some kinks. The resulting pop was loud enough for Anthony to hear. Sighing, Jason went on. "I saw something up there."

"What?"

"Something in the hall mirror. A face."

Anthony finished his beer and placed the empty bottle on the counter. "It's an old mirror, tarnished and probably in need of a good dusting. You've heard of matrixing? Where your mind tries to find familiar shapes out of chaos? I'm sure that's all it was. A weird anomaly in the reflection, and your mind just saw it as a face."

"It was there. Very clear. Just for a second, and then it was gone. But I saw it clearly." Jason rolled the cool bottle between his hands. "An older man with dark hair and bushy eyebrows. And a look of pure evil."

"Imagination, then." With a comforting smile, Anthony walked over and stood behind Jason. He began rubbing Jason's neck with practiced fingers. As usual, Jason's head lolled with the movement of Anthony's strong hands, and he moaned as the tension eased in his neck and shoulder muscles. "You came into this house filled with stories from your childhood, ghost stories and things that go bump in the night. You see some smudge in the mirror, and suddenly it's a scary face."

"Smudges don't have eyes that glare at you." Jason was beginning to calm down a little, and, while he wouldn't expect the pragmatic Anthony to just accept a ghostly image in a mirror without seeing it himself, he was slightly annoyed at his boyfriend's attitude. "I know what I saw. And then there was the room. I couldn't walk in. I felt like the floor was *pulling* me down. It was freaky."

"A dizzy spell. You said so yourself."

"That's because I knew you wouldn't believe that the room, for all intents and purposes, attacked me." Jason thought he was doing pretty well, keeping his tone level. And he wasn't really angry at Anthony. If the situation were reversed, he'd be skeptical as well. "Maybe it was a bad idea to move here."

"Your aunt left you the house in her will. I'm sure she wanted you to live here."

Jason drank some of his beer and then chuckled. "She and my dad didn't get along, which is why we never came back here after I was nine or so. I don't think I've said ten words to her in the past five years. She probably knew the place was filled to the attic with ghosts and left it to me to get back at our side of the family."

"It's an old Victorian house," Anthony said as he leaned forward and quickly kissed the top of Jason's head. "Bound to have a ghost or two. They'll get used to us, and we'll get used to them."

"You don't believe in ghosts."

"True, so that will make it easy for me." Anthony finished the neck rub and crossed over to the old refrigerator in the corner of the kitchen. He got out another beer and popped open the cap. "Seriously, though, we'd never be able to afford this place on what we make. Not right now, anyway. And it came furnished! We can get rid of the stuff that's too old or too old lady and make it our own." He pulled out the chair opposite Jason and sat down, taking a long pull at his beer as he plopped his butt into the seat. "It's perfect!"

"You didn't see that face." Jason's words didn't come out as strong as he intended. Had it been his imagination? He was tired, and it had already been a long day, and it wasn't even dinnertime.

"Hey, if any ghosts bother you, just tell them I'll beat the shit out of them if they continue to annoy you." Anthony's grin was infectious, and Jason found himself smiling as well.

"I'm sure that'll scare the crap out of them."

"Isn't that what they say to do on those TV shows where they hunt ghosts? To take back your house?" Anthony glanced around the room, a mocking sneer on his lips. "You hear me, ghosts? Leave my boyfriend alone! You tangle with him, and you tangle with me, and believe me, you don't want that!" He arched an eyebrow at Jason. "How's that?"

"I'm sure it worked. They're shaking in their shrouds."

"Seriously, though. Are you okay?"

Jason sighed. "I think so. I've just never had anything like that happen to me before. I was so *sure* that I saw a face… and the room…. I don't know. Maybe I'm just tired."

"Why don't you just rest, and I can get the rest of the boxes in?"

"No, I'm fine. Besides, I don't want to still be living in boxes by Thanksgiving."

A loud chime sounded, and Jason and Anthony looked at each other in confusion. "Doorbell," Anthony said. "Were we expecting anybody?"

Shaking his head, Jason replied, "Maybe Frank and Darren changed their minds and decided to help us. Or maybe it's the neighborhood welcoming committee." He chuckled. "Or maybe, now that almost everything has been moved inside, your son has decided he now has time to help out."

Anthony grinned as he rose. "That's doubtful. He'll be at Mom's until tomorrow, at least. He'll want to make sure we've got everything unpacked so he doesn't have to take time away from playing video games. It's probably our neighbors, who are about to find out that the newbies are a couple of fags. I hope they're cool about it. I'd hate to have to skin some of the neighborhood brats for spray-painting 'fag' on our mailbox."

They went to the front door together. Opening it, they found a woman who appeared to be in her late twenties or early thirties standing there, brandishing a large Tupperware container. At her side was a boy, perhaps ten or twelve, his face eager. The woman smiled.

"Hello there!" She seemed slightly embarrassed. "We're your neighbors from across the way. Number 178." She indicated the house with a twist of her head. "The one with the picket fence. I'm Maureen, and this is Charlie."

Charlie looked like he wanted to dart past his mother and run into the house. The boy's bright eyes were looking past Anthony and Jason as if they didn't even exist. The kid just wanted to see what lay beyond the threshold, and Jason found himself chuckling. "I'm Jason, and this is Anthony." Should he have said boyfriend, made it obvious? Probably not, not with the kid there. Besides, he was sure Maureen was catching on. "We were just making coffee," he lied. "Would you care to come in and join us?"

"Oh, we can't stay. I just wanted to bring you this," she said, presenting them with the container. "It's a pineapple upside-down cake. You know, a sort of welcome to the neighborhood."

"Can't we go in?" Charlie asked.

His mother smiled indulgently at him. "I'm sure they have things to do. Perhaps some other time, Charlie."

"Really," Anthony said. He even opened the door a few inches wider to show that the invitation was genuine. "We were taking a break anyway."

Maureen handed Jason the cake. "We really can't. I just wanted to say hi and," she said with a slight blush, "get a look at you. You know how neighbors are. Gotta be nosy! I'm sure you'll be very happy here. And don't worry about getting the Tupperware back to me right away. Believe me, I've got cabinets full of the stuff!"

"Well," Jason said, somewhat disappointed that she didn't seem to want to come inside. It would have been nice to get to know at least one of their neighbors. Plus it would be an excuse not to hoist more boxes upstairs to that damned room. "If you're sure. But, seriously, come by anytime."

"Oh, we will," Maureen promised. She turned and tried to guide Charlie into coming with her, but the boy balked.

"But I want to see the ghosts!" he cried.

"WELL, WE won't be the two gays that moved into the area," Anthony said as he stood in the side room they had already dubbed the library, due to the large bookcases filled with dusty tomes. There was a fireplace and several wingbacked chairs, giving the room a cozy, old-world feel. Even the lamps, with the once-colorful shades and ornate stands, made it seem like a room pulled right out of a gentleman's club in London. Not that Anthony had ever been in such an establishment, but he could envision Mycroft Holmes standing before the fire, awaiting news from his brother, Sherlock, who was involved in some important case. "We're going to be the guys that moved into the haunted house."

It was evening, and all the boxes had been transferred inside. Those that were marked for upstairs were in the middle bedroom, awaiting unpacking. Jason had placed the ones he'd carried just outside the door, and Anthony had put them into the room. Anthony didn't comment, but he noticed Jason had grown pale just coming close to that bedroom and made sure he didn't step one foot over the threshold.

Jason was sitting in one of the wingbacked chairs before the fireplace, as if feeling warmth from a fire that had burned there many years ago. They had opened a bottle of wine to celebrate moving into their new home, and Jason was on his second glass. He was holding his wine close to his mouth but not drinking and staring at the empty hearth.

Anthony examined some of the volumes on the shelf in front of him. "Your aunt seemed to have had ghosts on her mind. Have you looked at these books? *Poltergeist Phenomena. The Psychic Dead.* That sounds like a fun read. *Spirits and Necromancy.*" He pulled out a thin book with a blue cover. "*Death is Not the End.* Well, that's a comforting thought." He replaced the book and checked out another shelf. "Oh, here's *Wuthering Heights.* Personally, I think I'd rather read *Spirits and Necromancy.* Heathcliff and Catherine gave me a headache when we had to read about them in school." He glanced over at Jason, who seemed not to have moved a muscle. "You're awfully quiet."

Jason jerked into motion, taking a sip of wine and then setting the glass down on the small table next to his chair. "Just thinking."

"About?"

"You don't want to know."

Anthony, a thin smile on his face, strode over to stand next to Jason. He stroked his boyfriend's thinning hair gently. "That face?"

Jason nodded.

"It bothered you that much?"

"I just wish I really knew if I saw it or not. I was so sure. I can still see every detail."

"Hey," Anthony said, leaning down to kiss Jason's forehead. "If this place turns out to be haunted, we'll deal with it. Move if we have to. Sell the place."

"You mean that?"

"Well, it's really not up to me. Your aunt left it to you, not me. But, yeah. I want you to be happy, and you're not going to be if scary faces are going to be popping up and frightening you left, right, and center. We can find an apartment, although I'd hate to give this up. I've always wanted to live in a big house like this." Anthony moved over to the fireplace and ran a finger over the mantle, picking up a layer of dust. "Clean this up, and we've got our own little *Downton Abbey.*"

"Oh," Jason said with a grin, "can we hire an evil, scheming maid?"

"Two, if you like." Anthony was enjoying seeing Jason smile again. "Seriously, though, I know you believe in ghosts and stuff like that, but if they do exist, they can't hurt you. At least, that's what they say."

"The face I saw, he looked like he'd give it a good go."

Anthony turned and was about to speak when something caught his eye. A blue book was lying on the floor a few feet away from the bookcase. "That's funny. I'm sure I put that back on the shelf." He went over and picked up the book, frowning as he examined the cover once more. "*Death Is Not the End.*"

"YOU COMING to bed or what?" Anthony asked, already slipping between the sheets.

"In a minute," Jason replied. He was in the bathroom, just having finished brushing his teeth. The mirror over the sink was situated so he could see part of the bedroom, and he smiled as he saw Anthony attempt to cover his legs with the sheets as quickly as possible. *He doesn't want me to see that he's still wearing his socks.* Jason shook his head. He knew Anthony was embarrassed over his toenail fungus and hardly ever went without his feet being covered, but Jason couldn't care less. So his toenails looked gnarly? Big deal! Jason loved the whole package, flaws and all.

Maybe I should say something, Jason thought. He decided against it. It was a conversation they'd had several times, and Jason's assurances that he didn't find Anthony's toes repulsive didn't seem to be getting through his boyfriend's defenses. *Maybe I can get him to a doctor that he'll listen to. Make the doctor the bad guy, not me.*

Jason wiped the remaining foam from his mouth and turned off the bathroom light. He padded quickly across the room to the bed, his feet feeling chilled from the hardwood floor. He slid in next to Anthony, shivering slightly. "Is the heat on? It's positively frigid in here!"

Anthony turned, enfolding Jason in his arms. "I think it is. Might not be set on a decent temperature, though. I'll check it out in the morning."

Jason snuggled up close to his boyfriend, enjoying the body heat from Anthony's warm skin. He was about to say something else about the chilly room, but Anthony seemed to have other ideas. As soon as Jason opened his mouth, Anthony leaned in and kissed him passionately. The first word of the sentence Jason had attempted to say became a short sound that quickly turned into a moan. Their tongues met, and Anthony pulled Jason even closer. Without breaking off the kiss, Anthony maneuvered himself until he was on top of Jason.

Their hands began to roam, and Jason soon had one of his down the back of Anthony's boxer shorts. He began to knead the soft flesh of his lover's buttocks and was rewarded by Anthony writhing on top of him. Jason could feel Anthony's erection pressing up against his thigh. Anthony snaked out an arm and switched off the bedside lamp, plunging the room into near darkness. The blinds were closed over the window, but they were old, and several slats were broken, allowing in the moonlight.

Jason relinquished his grasp on Anthony's ass and ran his hands down his lover's back. They kissed again, briefer this time but no less passionate. Halfway through the kiss, though, Anthony seemed to freeze. He stopped squirming and ceased exploring the inside of Jason's mouth with his tongue. The paralysis, whatever the cause, was only momentary, and soon Anthony was again grinding against Jason's body and kissing him with an almost animalistic passion.

Anthony ran his fingers through Jason's short hair. He paused, as if surprised there wasn't enough hair there to grasp. He slid his mouth sideways, now kissing Jason's cheek before moving to his ear. He nibbled Jason's earlobe and murmured, "Ben."

"What?" Jason was puzzled.

"I want you," Anthony whispered, his voice husky. "I want to be inside you."

"No, but you called me Ben."

Anthony raised his head so he could gaze into his boyfriend's eyes. "No, I didn't."

"Yes, you did. I heard you plainly. You said Ben."

Smiling, Anthony resumed stroking Jason's hair. "It's nothing."

"Nothing? You just called me by the wrong name. Who's Ben? Was he an ex you haven't told me about?" Jason thought that unlikely. After all, he knew about Anthony's failed teenage marriage with a girl who turned out to be a drug addict. The only good thing that had come out of that mess had been Gary. Shortly after Gary's birth, Anthony's wife had run off, never to be heard from again. If Anthony had told him all that, surely there wasn't any romantic indiscretion he'd hidden from his lover.

Anthony chuckled, but it seemed to Jason there was a hint of guilt in Anthony's brown eyes. "I don't even know a Ben. You misheard me."

"I don't think so," Jason said. Something was wrong, and it wasn't just Anthony's name mistake. Anthony was a quiet lover, preferring to speak little, if at all. Saying things like "I want to be inside you" just wasn't Anthony. Jason frowned. "Are you feeling okay?"

"I feel fine."

"It's just that… I don't know. You're acting weird."

"I tell you, I'm fine." Anthony's voice came out as a growl. "Now, Ben, are we going to screw, or are we going to chat all night?"

Now Jason was alarmed. "You did it again! You called me Ben!"

There was an ugly twist in Anthony's grin. "Why wouldn't I? It's your name."

Jason's heart felt like it had been dipped in ice water. He slid out from under Anthony as gently as he could, trying not to notice the annoyed glance his boyfriend was giving him. "I don't know what's wrong here," Jason said, turning onto his side away from Anthony, "but I don't think we should be doing this."

Anthony twisted until he was back on his side of the bed, looking up at the ceiling. He was silent for nearly a minute. When he finally spoke, the harshness had vanished, and he sounded like the Anthony Jason had known for years. "I don't know what came over me," he said quietly. He placed a gentle hand on Jason's shoulder. "I'm sorry."

"It's okay," Jason replied, his voice slightly muffled by the pillow. "You're probably just tired from all the moving." It struck him that he was repeating Anthony's words to him earlier in the day, after the mirror incident. And Jason didn't think there was any truth to either statement.

ANTHONY SMILED encouragingly as his son, Gary, looked through the car window at the Victorian monstrosity he was to call home. "It looks like that house on *American Horror Story*," the boy said glumly.

"It looks nothing like that house," Anthony replied as he shut off the motor. "You're going to love this place. There's a room that I think would be a perfect rec room. You could have your game consoles hooked up to a big-ass TV in there, and we can get a pool table—"

"I don't know how to play pool."

"You can learn. Foosball, whatever you want. Your own little getaway. And wait until you see your room. Believe me, in a couple of days, you won't want to ever leave this place."

Gary leaned his head down to get a better look at the top of the house. There were several gables, and the roof sported a rooster weathervane. Anthony followed Gary's gaze, noticing for the first time the N for north was missing.

"Are there kids around here?" Gary asked.

"What do you mean? Of course there are kids! We met one yesterday, came over with his mom. Charlie, I think his name was." Anthony thought it best not to mention that Charlie was probably several years Gary's junior. "And you're closer to your school. You could walk there if you want."

Glumly, Gary fumbled at the door handle. "Sounds fantastic. A trek to school through mountains of snow."

Anthony flashed his son an encouraging smile. "Just wait," he said, hoping his enthusiasm for the house was infectious.

Anthony had to admit, however, that he was beginning to have doubts about the home. He was *sure* he'd put that book properly back in place, and it had ended up on the floor as if it had flown out of the bookcase on its own. And then there was his and Jason's aborted attempt at lovemaking. Anthony still wasn't sure what had come over him. Now the incident seemed foggy in his mind like a distant memory.

He was letting Jason's talk of ghosts get the better of him.

Not wanting to frighten his son, Anthony kept his tone light. "Maybe once you've got your room sorted and most of your stuff where you want it, we can watch a DVD or something. I got that James Bond movie. We haven't watched that yet."

The boy shrugged as he swung the passenger door open. "That might be cool." He got out of the car slowly, staring up at one of the upstairs windows as if something had caught his eye. He blinked and squinted his eyes.

Anthony noticed his son wasn't following him up to the house. "What is it? Something wrong?"

"I thought I saw someone in an upstairs window."

"Jason. He took a day off today to work on unpacking stuff."

Gary shook his head. "This guy was younger. And there was something weird about him. It was like his face was covered in blood. I only saw him for a second, but—"

Anthony put an arm around Gary's shoulders. "You, young man," he said, "have been watching too many scary movies." They took a few steps toward the front porch before Anthony paused. "Hey, wait a minute. You shouldn't be watching *American Horror Story.* Way too adult for you! When did you watch that?"

"At Grammy's. It's on Netflix!"

Anthony frowned. "I'm going to have to have words with your grandmother."

GARY FOUND the next few hours taxing. His dads were great—Jason had made him cocoa, and Anthony had given him a new PlayStation game—but Gary noticed they were going out of their way to paint their new home in rosy hues. No one was talking about the creepy feelings one got whenever you walked near the middle bedroom upstairs, or the odd sounds that seemed to come from not only the walls but the floors and ceilings as well. Like someone was walking around, just waiting to pop out and scare you.

After they'd left him in his new bedroom, to "put everything where you want it," as Jason had said, Gary had shoved a few things into the positively ancient chest of drawers and then decided the rest could wait. He sat on his bed—which, he had to admit, was larger and more comfortable than his old one—and looked around, trying to decide where his posters should go and if his Justice League action figures should be arranged on the old chest of drawers or on the shelf over his desk—*his* desk, one of the few items in the room that had been his in the old apartment.

Over the desk, Gary decided. Definitely.

He frowned as his ears picked up a sound, a soft tapping that seemed to be coming from the floorboards. *Great,* he thought, *the house has mice.*

No, this was a rhythmic tapping. Like someone was keeping beat to a tune in their head.

Or trying to get my attention.

One of the ghosts, maybe. Because Gary had already decided his new home was not only haunted, but Super Freaking Haunted, like on that TV show that had given him a few nightmares, not that he'd admit such a thing aloud. It hadn't been Jason he'd seen in the window, of that, Gary was certain. It had been a ghost. One that had died horribly. *That's why he was covered in blood,* Gary thought with a tiny shiver of glee.

Maybe this house was going to be all right after all. He could invite his friends over to play, and the ghosts would scare the shit out of them. And think of the Halloween parties!

The tapping came again, but this time it seemed to be coming right from under Gary's feet.

Something really was trying to get his attention. Gary rose, a small smile playing across his lips. It looked like it was time to do some exploring and see what this haunted house had to offer.

Maybe I'll see that bloody guy again. Gary's heart began to beat faster as he sifted through a few boxes that hadn't been unpacked until he located his flashlight, the one he sometimes used to read comic books under the covers at night. The one thing he knew from watching horror movies was that you *never* went exploring in a haunted house without a flashlight. Ghosts liked it dark.

Gary crept downstairs, trying to make as little noise as possible, which wasn't easy with the creaky staircase. He could hear his dad and Jason talking in the kitchen, but if they heard him coming downstairs, they didn't pay him any attention. That was okay with Gary. He wanted to check out the place on his own.

Earlier, his dad had given him a tour of the place and had pointed out a door that led to the basement. They hadn't gone down there. His dad had laughed and said, "It's a bit dirty. Loads of spiders and cobwebs. It's going to take weeks to clean it up." What better place for ghosts than a cobwebby basement?

The door squeaked with protest as Gary opened it, and he felt cold air come up and wash over him. Cold, musty air.

Gary found a light switch and flicked it. Nothing. *Good thing you brought the flashlight.* With a sense of equal parts dread and excitement, Gary traveled down the steps, his flashlight beam showing him the way. He was reminded of that time he'd gone to Kings Island amusement park with his dads and they'd taken him on his first roller coaster. Yes, he was afraid, but he was thrilled as well. He wanted to see a ghost, but part of him wanted to run back upstairs and snuggle next to his dad while they watched James Bond shoot up some bad guys.

"Hello?" Gary felt a little silly speaking out loud. Did he really expect an answer?

In a way, he wouldn't have been surprised if there had been. The basement—what he could see of it—was old, creepy, dusty, and full of cobwebs… but it felt *occupied.*

Gary allowed his beam to wander around the main part of the basement. There were doors leading to other areas and what looked like an old coal room to his left, but he could check those out some other time. Right now he felt like what he was looking for was here somehow, waiting for him.

"Anyone here?" Gary felt the tiny hairs on the back of his neck bristling.

Was that someone chuckling?

Suddenly, Gary wanted to be anywhere but in that dark, dank basement. He turned to head back up the stairs, but as he moved, his flashlight caught something on one of the walls. Writing. He swung the light beam back. *Holy crap.*

He hadn't been mistaken. Someone had written on the wall in red—blood? Two words.

YOU'RE MINE.

Reading the words, Gary felt a chill in his bones. He wanted to scream, but somehow his throat wouldn't work. And then his flashlight beam faltered and went out. Gary whimpered and shook the damn thing. Finally the light returned.

The wall was bare now. No words in red.

Gary went back upstairs as fast as his legs would take him.

CHAPTER 2

I FELT like I had been in the closet for years.

I looked at my watch, the one Robbie had given me for my birthday right before he died. The luminous dial told me I'd only been standing there for twenty minutes. Honestly, it seemed much longer. Okay, maybe not years, but at least an hour.

That was the trouble with the detective business. Sometimes you had to wait. Your usual private detective often had to wait in his car outside some woman's house to see who entered. I was waiting for an incubus to attack. Well, we can't all specialize in divorce work. I specialized in weird.

I sighed and peeked out through the crack I'd left in the door so I would have a fairly good view of the bed. The room was pretty dark, but I could just make out the jumble of blonde hair on the pillow. The only sound coming from the room was the ticking of the alarm clock on the bedside table, which seemed to be extraordinarily loud. I wondered how my client, Penny, could sleep with that racket going on. She must be used to it. Ticktock, ticktock. I'd have thrown the fucker across the room, had it been my clock.

Of course, it wasn't Penny in the bed at the moment. My decoy was in her place. Penny was at a Motel 6 down the road, hopefully sleeping soundly in the knowledge that her nocturnal troubles were being taken care of by Duncan Andrews, private eye and killer of incubi. I'm such a poet.

My stomach growled. Loudly. That wouldn't do. You have to catch incubi at just the right moment, and if they hear unsettled tummy noises coming from the closet... well, it gives the game away. Mentally, I told my stomach to shut up. It replied with another gurgle, much softer this time.

I leaned against the wall, careful not to hit any of the clothes hanging on the rail. I made some movements with my mouth, twisting it one way and then another, but I found that didn't entertain me much. Ticktock, ticktock. I thought about several different ways of smashing that damned clock. I had just imagined hiding it in a watermelon right before a Gallagher show—was he even still around?—when a sound from the bedroom brought me to full attention. It had been a scrape at the window.

Showtime.

I stood straight, alert, and tightened the grip of the .38 in my left hand. More sounds came from the bedroom as the window was slowly shoved upward. Then came some shuffling as the incubus climbed inside. Finally, he came into view.

An incubus is a demon that, to put it bluntly, lives off screwing. They can alter their appearance and look like Brad Pitt if they think that will get them some nookie. They're at their most powerful when they're horny, but this is also the only time they can be destroyed. A silver bullet right through their heart will make them go bye-bye, but they have to be standing erect and proud, so to speak. Hell of a demon design flaw, but at least they go out smiling.

This incubus wasn't bothering with putting on the good looks. He was human in appearance, but only just. In the meager light, he appeared to be a very, very old man with gray, wrinkled skin dotted with liver spots. There were a few tufts of white hair sticking out of the top of his skull, but you'd hardly call it a ravishing hairstyle. He was wearing a ratty robe, dark in color, that was open, giving me a great view of his junk.

I'll say this for incubi: they're hung like horses. This guy was no exception. It was an odd contrast—this old, gnarled dude with sagging skin with a big old stiffy sticking out like a curved dagger ready to impale its prey. He could have gone into an Internet chat room claiming ten inches, and he wouldn't have been exaggerating. An accompanying picture, though, would have been a bad idea. Not a looker, even if you're into nonagenarians.

The incubus approached the bed. It looked to me like he was slobbering a little, but that could have been just the bad lighting. I could clearly see him reach out to the figure under the covers, though. His hand shook a little with anticipation as he pulled back the bedcovers.

He snarled as he realized that the recumbent figure wasn't Penny, but a blow-up doll I'd purchased earlier that day at a sex shop. I got one with lifelike hair because I like to keep my incubi happy.

I kicked open the closet door and emerged, .38 pointed right at the ugly sucker. I had to get him while he was still fully engorged, and didn't want to give his stiffy a chance to deflate, even though it was fun watching the shocked expression on his face.

"Dumbass," I said as I pulled the trigger. Only a horny, stupid incubus would fall for the old blow-up doll in the bed trick.

The bullet hit the mark. The incubus flew back, his arm taking out the bedside lamp as he fell. I knew I'd hit his heart but came around the bed and stood over him to make sure. There was a lovely hole in his chest with wafts of black smoke billowing out. He was writhing about a little and choking on the black blood filling his mouth and spilling out onto Penny's nice baby-blue carpet. I aimed and shot him again, this time in the crotch. It wouldn't kill him any faster, but it was fun for me, so what the hell.

Finally, the incubus lay still and began to dissolve. Soon he'd be nothing more than a black pile of ick on the rug, but I didn't need to stick around for that. One more dead demon. I loved my job sometimes.

"SO HOW are you and Robbie doing?" Gina asked.

We were sitting in her parlor around a little table, drinking tea. The table had a dark-blue cloth on it but, thankfully, no crystal ball. That was for the other parlor, the one for the tourists and Gina's regular clients. It was full of new-age paraphernalia and where Gina told fortunes for anyone willing to cross her palm with silver. She also took

Visa and MasterCard. This room was more understated, and it even had a television set, which was on, although the sound was down. On it, Ellen DeGeneres was interviewing a guest, some handsome guy I probably should have recognized but didn't. They looked like they were having a good time.

"Fine," I answered.

Gina arched an eyebrow. "Really?"

"Really." I took a sip of tea. It tasted faintly of peppermint. "Is this just tea? Not some witchy brew that makes one reveal one's soul?"

She smiled. "Now, would I do that to you?"

"In a heartbeat, if you thought it would work."

I was boasting, as a potion from Gina definitely would work on me or anyone else, for that matter. Gina told fortunes for a living but had the inside track. She was a witch, and I'm not talking about your everyday Wiccan here, but an honest-to-goodness spell-casting sorceress who'd lived for several hundred years already. I wasn't about to ask her actual age because you want to be careful insulting someone who can literally turn you into a newt, but I estimated she was 330 years old, give or take a decade or two. I was basing my guess on the knowledge that she'd been a child at the time of the Salem witch trials, but maybe real witches stay children longer than regular humans, so I could be way off.

Whatever her age, Gina looked good. She appeared to be in her late twenties, early thirties, and had long blonde hair and striking blue eyes. She rarely dressed in anything other than black, and today was no exception. She even had a black lacy shawl sort of thing wrapped around her shoulders to ward off the chill in the room. It seemed a bit old-fashioned, but considering she was older than the Constitution, old-fashioned was allowed.

"If I was using some spell to make you bare your soul," she said with a sly grin, "what would you tell me about you and Robbie?"

I was about to give some glib response but stopped and switched to honesty. Maybe there was something in the tea after all. "I don't know. We're getting along great, probably better than we have for years. Not that we weren't getting along before, mind you."

"Of course not."

"I presume he's still planning on leaving at New Year's. We don't talk about it, through mutual consent."

Gina twisted her head to the side, giving me that look psychiatrists on TV give when they're sure their clients aren't being entirely truthful. "The way you use the word 'presume' tells me you don't think he's going to go."

"Should I lie down on the couch while you get out your pad and pencil?" When she smiled to show me she got the reference, I went on. "But you're right. I'm not convinced. I think he'll find an excuse to stay on longer. How much longer, I don't know. We've battled this thing for over ten years now, and we've always just taken things one day at a time. I know he'll eventually move on, but I think it will be when both of us are ready."

Having a boyfriend who is a ghost has major drawbacks, and it's something I don't recommend. Luckily, most people can't see ghosts, at least not all the time. Like that kid in the Bruce Willis movie, I saw them every day. At the grocery store. At the bank. I once even saw John Belushi up at Second City in Chicago, and let me tell you, that was one unfunny ghost. Being dead can make some people a little pissy.

Robbie was completely at ease with being a spirit. We were good together when he was alive and not bad after his death. There were, like I said, drawbacks, though. The lack of sex being the biggest. He could sometimes muster up enough energy to become solid enough for a kiss or a quick grope, but not more than that. So that sucked. Also, he still looked like he was twenty while I was getting some gray nestling in there with the dark hair. Not a lot. Just enough to make me go "ugh."

Feeling that he was holding both of us back from getting on with our lives—well, life in my case, death in his—Robbie had recently decided that on New Year's Eve, he was finally going to move on and journey to the other side.

We had a screwy relationship, and maybe he was right. Maybe we were holding each other back. But then again, who was to say? Maybe we were still together because it was meant to be that way. Sure, it was frustrating, not being able to be physical with him, but I knew that if he really did go, something inside me would die as well. And I didn't know if I could handle that.

Gina seemed to be reading my thoughts. "You're in denial about this whole thing, aren't you?"

"Yep."

"Do you think that's good?"

I shrugged. "It's the only way I can cope with the idea. Ignore it. Maybe it'll go away. Maybe he really won't go to the other side come the end of the year—and if that happens, I'll try really hard not to say I told you so—but if he does, I'll deal with it then."

She smiled gently and placed her hand on mine. "You're predictable, at least."

DAISY WAS ravenous when I got home, so a trip to the park was in order. Having a bulldog that was a zombie could be almost as difficult as having a boyfriend who was a ghost, especially when her preferred meal was squirrel. You'd think by now that all the squirrels in the park would know to scatter when the odd-looking dog with the bloodshot eyes was around, but somehow, some of them seemed to have missed the memo.

Robbie was with us, looking a little pale but fairly substantial. He was wearing torn jeans and a football jersey. My jeans had no rips, and I had my leather jacket on. Not being dead, I could feel the cold November winds. As we pulled into the park, and I maneuvered into a parking space, Daisy, unable to contain her excitement, scrabbled into the front seat and tried to jump into Robbie's lap. Robbie not being solid enough, she went right through him, her legs sinking right through his. If this bothered her, she didn't show it. She was too focused on a squirrel she had spotted on the side of a nearby tree.

Once the car was parked, Robbie attempted to open the door for Daisy, but his fingers went right through the door handle. "Shit," he said. "You'll have to do the honors."

I leaned over and opened the door. Daisy shot out like she hadn't eaten in weeks, making a mad dash for the closest squirrel. Unfortunately, this one was smart enough to dart farther up the tree, out of reach from the slobbering chops of my undead dog. Daisy came to a halt at the bottom of the tree and stared up at the squirrel, as if willing it to fall or be stupid enough to come back down.

"You're a little on the transparent side tonight," I said as I got out myself. Robbie just went through the door.

"Conserving my energy. You said we'd go see that new Johnny Depp movie at the mall tonight."

It was true, I had, although I was already beginning to regret making the offer. Taking Robbie to a place where there were lots of people was always risky. Not many people could see ghosts, but in a big crowd, there would usually be someone who had some ability. They may not be able to see him clearly, but they'd see a shadow or a misty figure. "It's had mixed reviews," I said, not untruthfully.

"We don't have to see that one. I'm sure we can find something else. Maybe something where they blow a lot of shit up."

I closed the car door. "My boyfriend, the movie connoisseur."

Robbie grinned. "I'm like a dead Roger Ebert."

"Roger Ebert's dead too."

"Is he? Funny. Haven't seen him at any of the meetings."

Robbie was joking. Ghosts didn't really have meetings. Not that they'd told me about, anyway. We ambled around the park for a while, keeping half an eye on Daisy to make sure she wasn't getting into mischief. The only other people in the park were two teenage boys playing Frisbee, and they were too far off to notice some of the park's squirrel population was meeting a particularly nasty end. Squirrel! Chomp! That was my dog. Sometimes I wondered what it would be like to have a normal life.

Daisy, having had her fill of squirrel heads, came romping over to us. There was a little blood and gore around her chops, so I took out a cloth I carried to the park for just such a purpose and wiped her mouth. She wagged her tail happily. I wondered if she knew she was different

Dead End

from other dogs. I also wondered what would happen as she aged. Since she was undead, would bits of her start rotting and falling off? I'd have to ask Gina sometime. After all, she was the one who'd resurrected Daisy in the first place. Hopefully she knew the consequences of what she was doing. Would I end up with a one-eyed, three-legged zombie bulldog hobbling after decrepit squirrels at some point?

The ringing of my cell phone interrupted my ruminations. I answered as I tucked the now bloody rag back into my pocket. "Hello."

"I was wanting to speak with Duncan Andrews," the caller said.

"You're in luck. What can I do for you?"

There was a pause. I'm used to pauses when people call me. Usually they have a problem no one else can handle, one they're not even sure they believe is happening in the first place. I didn't exactly advertise that I specialized in cases involving ghouls, demons, vampires, and whatnot, but word got around. Because, let's face it, when your Aunt Bertha had been turned into a newt by a pissed-off sorcerer, the Indianapolis Police Department just weren't going to be able to handle it.

"This is going to sound weird." Another pause, longer this time.

"I like weird. Tell me more," I prompted.

"Actually, you and I have met before," the caller said, changing the subject abruptly to something less difficult to find words for. "At my cousin's funeral. You used to date him, I believe."

Well, I still was, in that strange living-person-dating-a-ghost kind of way, but he didn't need to hear that. "You're Robbie's cousin?" I asked. My query made Robbie, who had been tossing sticks for Daisy to fetch, stop and stare at me.

"Yeah. You may not remember me. Jason Church. We didn't really chat much."

I'd talked little at Robbie's funeral and had only a vague recollection of meeting anyone. Robbie, a questioning frown on his face, touched my elbow and mouthed the words, "Is that Jason?" It was

25

doubtful Jason would have been able to hear him even if he'd spoken aloud, but old habits died hard. I nodded to Robbie.

"What can I do for you, Jason?" I asked.

"I think.... I don't know. I think we have a ghost in our house." Jason's words were accompanied by a dry, mirthless chuckle. "And I think it's trying to kill us."

CHAPTER 3

"I was only ever in that house once," Robbie said. "I was just a little kid, but even then, I hated being there. It just had that feel to it, you know? That something evil was there. Not out in the open, but in the woodwork. Lurking just out of your vision."

We were back at our place, seated around the kitchen table. Well, Gina, Nick, and I were seated. Robbie was leaning against the wall, and Daisy was snoozing in her favorite chair in the living room. I'd opened a bottle of pinot grigio, and we were sipping and wondering what this new case would bring. Robbie, unable to enjoy the wine, just eyed the bottle with a wistful sigh.

"Sounds pretty simple to me," I said. "Go in there, figure out who's doing the haunting, exorcise his ass, and go home. Couple hours' work."

"We should definitely try to get him, or her, to move on first," Nick chimed in. "Give them a chance to leave of their own accord."

Nick was new to the I-Can-See-Ghosts Club and was the champion of the notion of getting spirits to depart of their own free will. Sort of the Dr. Phil of the paranormal world. By day, he taught history to a bunch of teenagers who didn't know Attila the Hun from Napoleon. When the sun went down, though, he donned tights and a cape and went around fighting crime. Wait, that was Batman. Nick just talked with ghosts and let them know they could pass on to the other side if they wanted.

"I'm meeting with Robbie's cousin in an hour," I said after consulting the Felix the Cat clock on the wall. I hated that thing, but Robbie thought it was cute. "If possible, I'll arrange for us to go to the house tonight, and we can see what the score is. Maybe we can clear this up before *Saturday Night Live* comes on."

Robbie's face bore a wistful smile. "It'll be nice to see Jason again. Although, I got to be honest, I'm not looking forward to entering that house again. It was evil."

"Houses can't be evil."

"This one managed quite nicely."

I turned to Gina. "So what do you say? Make it a foursome?"

She shook her head. "I've got a date with Mark tonight, so you guys go along and have your fun. Anyway, there's not much I can do to help. Witches don't have power over spirits, at least for the most part, so I'd just be standing around twiddling my thumbs."

"Bring Mark along," I said, half-seriously. "It's time he spent more time with the gang, and since this case involves family, I'm sure it would be okay."

Gina smiled. "Funnily enough, wandering around a drafty house burning sage and telling some ghost to get the hell out isn't my idea of a hot date. We're going to the Churchill and then out dancing."

It may have been my imagination, but I thought I was getting a weird vibe from Gina, as if she was hiding something. Like Mark didn't want to spend time with our strange little gang, or Gina didn't want to involve him in our madness. It was only recently that Gina had told her boyfriend he was dating a centuries-old witch, and, to his credit, he'd taken the news pretty well. Still, he seemed like an outsider, and I didn't want to exclude someone who obviously meant something to Gina.

I looked again at Felix. His hands hadn't moved a lot since the last time I'd glanced his way. "Well, I'll go see Jason and arrange things. Let's assume, though, that we'll go to the house tonight and do some ghost zapping."

I wasn't expecting cheers as I got up, but I was mildly surprised by the looks on my friends' faces. Nick looked apprehensive, Gina seemed miles away, and Robbie appeared to be downright worried. Finally, Gina started to get up, but before she got to her feet, a violent shudder went through her body, one of those where you can see the person's shoulders hunching and their arms twitching. She shook it off and then looked at me, a hint of warning in her eyes.

"I wonder," she said slowly, "if this is going to be as easy as you seem to think."

JASON CHURCH looked like he hadn't slept in days. He wore a goatee that needed a trim, and he had dark circles around his eyes. He sat across the desk from me and seemed to have no idea how to start, so I thought I'd help him out.

"So you're living in a haunted house."

He almost smiled. Then he closed his eyes, took a deep breath, and opened his eyes again. "I've watched those ghost-hunting TV shows for years. I just never thought it was really true, you know. That stuff like that actually happens."

I nodded encouragingly.

Jason went on. "I guess it started the day we moved in. Anthony and Gary and me. Anthony's my boyfriend. He's a personal trainer. Gary's his son. He's fourteen." Jason favored me with an embarrassed smile. "Anthony had a couple of wayward years after high school. Got married to some girl who hated him, but they had a great kid. She's out of the picture now, so we've got Gary. He's cool." He was avoiding getting to the point, but that was okay by me. I had time.

"How long have you and Anthony been together?"

"Two years now. The three of us were living in my apartment on the east side when my aunt died, and I found out she left me her house."

"And things started to happen the first day?"

He bit his lip. "That was the first time I saw the face."

"What kind of face?"

Jason closed his eyes again. "It was horrible. Pure evil."

"Male, female? Old, young?"

"An older male, maybe in his fifties, if I had to guess." Jason looked at me, probably to see if he could find any hint in my face that I thought he was crazy. Not seeing anything of that sort, he continued. "There's an old mirror in the upstairs hallway. We were hauling in some boxes, and that's where I saw it. The eyes were like, I don't know, full of hatred. Red, blazing eyes. I saw it, plainly too. Anthony tried to tell me it was just imperfections in the surface of the mirror or some flaw in the backing, but I knew it wasn't."

"Have you seen the face since?"

"Several times. Always in that mirror."

That could be good. Maybe it was the mirror that was haunted. Get rid of the mirror, and we might get rid of the spirit.

The more Jason told me, though, the less likely that seemed. We talked for over an hour, and I heard about the times when it seemed Anthony was possessed by some entity, referring to Jason as Ben. I heard about footsteps in the night and how Anthony, after hearing them for several nights in a row, became convinced someone had actually broken into the house and was pacing up and down in the attic. A thorough search, however, had revealed the house was empty. Once he warmed to his subject and felt more comfortable, Jason poured out story after story. I'd heard similar tales before, of course, but even I could see that the house on Denmark Street was extremely active. It didn't seem to matter if it was day or night; practically every day, *something* odd happened. Sometimes it was something little, like walking into the kitchen to find all the cabinet doors open. Sometimes it was the frightening face in the mirror, though, or worse.

"One morning, we were having breakfast," Jason said. He was leaning forward in his seat, his elbows on his knees. "Just cereal. I poured the milk on mine, and it came out, no problem. Anthony went to pour his, and it came out in glops. Mine was perfectly fine, but in the few seconds between me pouring and him reaching for the milk, it had curdled!"

I frowned. "How long have you been living there?"

"We moved in three weeks ago."

That was a lot of activity for three weeks. "Can I ask why you're still living there? I mean, most people would have bolted by now."

"I've wanted to. I've brought it up to Anthony several times, and he keeps saying that if things keep on happening, he'll consider it. Anyway, last week I contacted a local ghost group. Hoosier Ghost Pact, they call themselves. I checked out their website, and they seemed legitimate."

"And what happened?"

"They came out last Friday night. They only stayed two hours. I don't know exactly what happened, because they were supposed to stay the night. There was a girl in the group who said she was psychic. When they left, she was in tears. I mean, she was seriously upset. One of the other guys had to help her out to their car because she was crying so hard she couldn't see where she was going. The leader of the group told me and Anthony that they couldn't help us but that he knew someone who could. He gave us your card. I couldn't place the name at first, but I knew it sounded familiar. Then it hit me. You were the guy that Robbie was so hot on. I don't know why I didn't remember you right away. You don't run into too many guys named Duncan."

I recalled, vaguely, meeting Jason at Robbie's funeral. He hadn't had the goatee then and had had more hair. He'd also had, if memory served, about twenty pounds extra back then. Having a boyfriend who was a personal trainer had its perks. "I think it's a more common name in Scotland. My grandfather was a Scot." Hey, we were family, in a weird sort of way. I felt like I could be a little more open with a client who was related to my late—but still around—lover. But I thought we should get back to the subject at hand. "I'd like to come out and check out your place. Would tonight be convenient?"

"Sure. Anytime." Jason spoke quickly, and I think he was so relieved that if I'd wanted to run straight out to his house, he'd have offered to drive.

"Let's say seven."

Jason nodded and then ran a hand first over his face and then through his hair, what there was of it. "I thought for sure you'd think I was crazy."

"I know crazy. You're not it."

We stood, and he offered me his hand. "See you tonight," he said.

I wasn't about to tell him his dead cousin would be coming with me. If I had, I don't think it would be his own sanity he'd be questioning.

ROBBIE RODE in the back seat, which he didn't like much, but with Nick tagging along, I insisted. Otherwise it looked like I was alone in the front, chauffeuring Nick around town. The house was close to downtown, in one of those strange neighborhoods where you had blocks of rundown houses, and then suddenly—boom!—you had six or seven painted ladies in a row, old Victorian houses that had been restored to their glory days. SUVs were parked in most of the driveways, and there were some boys playing hoops at the house next door, a floodlight enabling them to see their playing area. Despite the fact that the sun had long since gone down, there was a kid on a bike coming down the sidewalk when we parked. He slowed, eying us with suspicion. He looked at Nick and then me, and then at the house we'd parked in front of.

"You're going in there?" he asked.

I nodded. "Yep."

"You know it's got ghosts, right?"

"So I hear." I examined the kid. He had sandy hair and freckles. The freckles were so prominent that I could see them even though he was mostly in shadow. He looked like Andy Griffith would be popping around to take him to the fishing hole any day now.

The kid's eyes were wide. "Don't the ghosts scare you?"

"Ghosts don't scare me," I said, stealing a quick glance at Robbie.

"They don't scare me neither," the kid said, his skinny chest puffing out. "I wanna get in there and see them, but my mom says I shouldn't bother the guys that live there now."

Nick was beginning to make restless movements, as if to remind me that we weren't there to chat with little kids. Taking the hint, I began to make my way to the paved walk that lead up to the front door. "Your mom's probably right, kid," I said with a little wave of my hand meant to indicate the conversation was over.

The kid had other ideas. He raised his voice, hoping to halt our progress. "You know those guys are gay, right?"

I stopped and looked back. "Does that bother you?"

He made a face, one of those "whatever" looks. "Nah. Don't matter to me. Bothers some older people sometimes, though. That's what my mom says."

I hesitated, trying to figure out if the kid was referring to me as old. He didn't seem to be, so I let it go. "Well, we're expected, and we don't want to be late, so we'll have to talk some other time, kiddo."

"My name's Charlie."

"Mine's Duncan. This is Nick. We'll see you, Charlie."

Charlie wasn't done with us, though. "Are you here to get rid of the ghosts?"

I sighed. The kid was starting to get on my nerves. "Yeah."

Nick piped up. "Well, we're going to ask them to play nice first. If they won't, then we'll get rid of them."

"They won't," Charlie informed us. "I don't think they're very nice ghosts."

We said good-bye to Charlie and walked up the short path to the porch. In the dark, the house *did* look a little creepy, and the closer we got to it, the more my psychic sense began to tingle. I realized that, unconsciously, the ominous feeling I was getting from the house was causing me to slow my pace. I looked over at Nick, and he seemed to be getting the same impression. The house didn't seem to want us going in.

Or rather, *something* in the house didn't want us there. As I'd said earlier, there was no such thing as an evil house.

Although, walking up to 175 Denmark Street, I wasn't feeling too sure about that statement.

We paused before mounting the steps up to the porch, mainly because one of our numbers had halted dead in his tracks. Robbie was staring up at one of the upstairs windows. He was often pale—being a ghost, skin pigmentation wasn't always something that came through—but standing there, he looked like a character from a black-and-white movie had decided to walk off the screen and join us.

"You okay?" I asked.

He started to shake his head but changed it to a shrug. "Just not looking forward to going in there again."

"You'll get to see your cousin again," I said, trying to put a positive spin on things. "You haven't seen him in ages."

Nick had gone halfway up the steps and placed a hand on one of the porch pillars. "You can almost *feel* it! It's like... I don't know... the building itself has a power. Like electricity coursing through it."

"We'll soon find out," I said, going up the steps two at a time.

Before I got to the front door, however, the porch light came on and Jason opened the door. "We heard you pull up," he said. "Come on in!"

Nick went first, and by his body language, it seemed like he was forcing his legs to propel him forward. I followed and was surprised by the atmosphere in the foyer. Gone was the feeling of dread I'd been experiencing. Inside, it was bright and cheery and seemed perfectly normal. There were no skeletal hands reaching out of the walls or portraits on the wall with eyes that seemed to follow you. There was a rather worn carpet on the floor and an ornate table and hat stand that didn't seemed to match Jason's personality. I assumed they had been his aunt's.

Jason had closed the door after I'd entered, so Robbie had to go through it. He glanced at his cousin with mock irritation. "Thanks, cuz. Asshole."

Before us was a short hall and a staircase. An archway off to our right seemed to lead to a living room. The other doors were closed. Mounted on the walls there were lights that resembled candles and a lighted chandelier close to the stairs. It seemed like they had every light source lit.

Nick was gazing around as well and seemed surprised nothing ghostly was jumping out at him. "Nice place," he said.

"Thanks," Jason said with a smile. "It's a neat house when things are quiet."

I realized Jason hadn't met Nick, so I introduced him, calling him an associate. Well, it sounded better than saying he was a history teacher who recently learned how to see ghosts.

Robbie was staring at Jason, or rather, at the top of his head. "Jesus, dude, what happened to your hair? It used to be down to your shoulders!"

Nick glared at Robbie, no doubt temporarily forgetting Jason couldn't hear Robbie's admittedly rude comment. Jason caught Nick's glare and peered at the area where Robbie was standing, probably wondering if Nick had spotted a mouse or something.

I ignored them and reached out with my mind. Yes, there it was. In the background. Lurking. Waiting. Sizing us up.

It was somewhat like the bridge scenes on *Star Trek: The Next Generation.* I'd been rewatching old *Trek* on Netflix when I wasn't involved in a case, and I noticed they usually had a background hum for these scenes that was supposed to be the sound of the engines. You had to listen for it, though; otherwise it was just background noise. The spirit—or spirits—in the house was like that. There, but you had to really reach out to notice him. Or them. I was beginning to think we might be dealing with multiple entities. It wouldn't be easy for just *one* ghost to generate that much negative energy.

A young man came in from the other room, a robust and buff guy I assumed was the personal trainer. Jason made the introductions, and first I and then Nick shook his hand. He seemed like a nice guy, and he didn't do that "I want to show how strong I am so I'm going to try to crush your hand" handshake, which was good because I had a firm grip myself, and I liked to win. Anthony showed signs that the events in the house were taking their toll on him as well, but he seemed a little embarrassed when the subject came up.

"It's been a quiet night," Jason said with a nervous laugh. "Maybe he knew you were coming and decided to hide."

"Maybe," I said. More likely, he was gathering energy to make one hell of a statement.

Anthony shuffled his feet a little. "I've got to admit, I was a little reluctant to let Jason get in touch with you."

I raised an eyebrow. "Why is that?"

He avoided looking me in the eye. "I'm just not sure of what's really going on here."

I nodded. "Have you seen this face yourself?"

Anthony shook his head. "No, can't say I have."

Jason spoke up. "But you've seen other stuff. The cabinet doors in the kitchen all opening at once. You've heard the footsteps. You've seen things flying off shelves."

"Those could be tremors or something," Anthony replied, although he didn't sound convinced himself.

"Well," I said cheerily, "if it's nothing, then we'll soon know, and you won't be out anything. No ghost, no charge." I looked at Anthony. "I understand you have a son."

He nodded. "He's at a friend's house tonight. I didn't want to involve him in…" He waved his hands in the air. "… this."

"Has he had experiences?"

Anthony shrugged. "If he has, he hasn't said anything to us."

I rubbed my hands together to show I was ready. "Would you like to show us around?"

Jason led the way, taking us from room to room. The place was nicely furnished, with some rooms containing so many antiques and heirlooms it almost seemed like we were in a museum. Jason told us his aunt had kept most of the original furniture that had come with the place when she'd bought it, so many of the items dated from before 1900.

In the dining room was a long mahogany table someone had put a lot of time and effort into restoring. "This," Jason said, stroking the top with a loving hand, "is supposedly one of the original pieces. My uncle did a lot of work on it, replacing one of the legs and varnishing it. We don't use it on a day-to-day basis. We mostly eat in the kitchen. But we had planned to have some friends over for Thanksgiving. That is, before…." He grew quiet.

Thanksgiving was less than a week away. Jason's mention of the holiday reminded me I hadn't made any plans yet. Maybe I could throw something together and have Nick, Gina, and her beau Mark over for a feast. But then, considering my cooking skills, maybe I'd better not. Turkey, as a rule, should taste like turkey, not charred muskrat.

Robbie was still not over the change in Jason's appearance. He sidled up next to me as we stood around the table, his eyes not leaving his cousin's head. "He looks so old."

"He's our age," I said in a whisper I hoped our hosts couldn't hear. "It's just that you haven't seen him in years."

"Yeah, but… hell! Makes me wonder what I'd look like if I'd lived."

"A stud," I told him. "Just one who's a little older."

Anthony looked at me. "Something wrong?"

Oops. Caught. Nick wasn't standing so far from me, so I used him as my excuse. "Just seeing if Nick was picking up on anything."

Nick, now that all eyes were on him, flushed with embarrassment. "No. No, nothing. Every now and then… but no." He jerked his head suddenly.

I knew why. I felt it too. Something was about to happen.

And then we heard what sounded like someone pounding on a wall with a hammer. A really big hammer. It started from somewhere farther in the house but with each bang came closer and closer until it seemed like it was just outside the dining room.

"Someone's trying to get our attention," Robbie muttered.

I looked at Jason and Anthony. They had moved a little closer to each other, no doubt drawing some fortitude from each other. All the color had gone from Jason's face, and he seemed like his knees might give out, and he'd fall to the floor in a heap. Anthony just stared at the doorway, his body tense. If a tiny kitten suddenly popped in from the hall, I thought he'd turn and run screaming from the room.

We could see nothing out in the hall, but there was a heavy feeling in the air, and my senses were telling me something was there, waiting for us to make our move.

I like a challenge. "You guys stay here," I said. I tried to sound casual. I'm not sure I pulled it off.

I was closest to the doorway, anyway. Nick began to follow me, but I motioned for him to stay. Out in the hall, there was... nothing. Whatever had been banging on the walls, attempting to get our attention, was gone. I looked up at the ceiling. Something told me our entity had retreated back upstairs. "Show off!" I yelled.

I didn't get a reply, not that I expected one.

Returning to the dining room, I found Jason and Anthony in pretty much the same position, except now they were holding hands. Nick was biting his lip, and Robbie... well, it was hard to read his expression. If he were a living person, I'd think he had a stomachache and was feeling a bit faint. I addressed the homeowners. "Have you heard that banging before?"

Jason nodded. "Usually it's footsteps, and they can be really loud, but we heard the banging one night last week."

Anthony added, "It was late at night. Woke us up. I got up, thinking I'd find holes in the walls and plaster all over the floor. There was nothing, though."

"Well, whatever you've got here, it's really pissed off about something. That much is for sure." I was trying to sound reassuring, like this was a walk in the park for me, but the truth was I had never felt anything like the power I was feeling within that house. I'd dealt with literally hundreds of angry ghosts in my time, but this was somehow different. I felt it in my bones. "I think whatever it was is upstairs right now. I'd like to go up there, but I think you guys should stay down here. Is it okay if I finish the tour on my own?"

Jason and Anthony were too shaken to even think, it seemed. They looked at each other and, not seeing an answer in the other's face, turned their gaze to me and then Nick as if seeking guidance. In their defense, it did sound like Thor had just come down their hall, smacking his hammer against the wall every couple of feet.

Finally, Jason nodded. "Sure," he said.

It wasn't until I got to the stairs that I realized Nick and Robbie were tagging along, although neither one of them looked happy about it. I paused two steps up, looking back at Nick. "You don't have to come. I can do this on my own."

"I want to lend my support," he said in a hushed voice, as if we were in a library and didn't want to be reprimanded by the stern librarian.

I raised an eyebrow at Robbie and he shrugged. "What's he going to do, kill me again? Gotta admit, though, I've got the heebie-jeebies. You know how when you shiver and someone says a goose walked over your grave? Well, I actually have a grave, and it feels like a whole bunch of geese are marching all over that sucker." He made a puzzled face. "Dumb saying though. A goose walked over your grave. What the heck are geese doing in a cemetery, anyway?"

"Walking over graves, apparently." I led the way up the steps. It felt like there was a physical force lurking up above us, and each step I took was harder than the last.

Behind me, I heard Nick mutter, "I've never even heard that phrase."

"My mom used to say it all the time," Robbie said. I noticed he was using library voice as well. "I think she got it from her mom, so it might be a British thing."

I paused and glanced behind me briefly. "Guys," I said, "you're babbling." My voice sounded extraordinarily loud, maybe because I wasn't using hushed tones.

"Sorry," Nick said.

Reaching the top step, I felt like I'd conquered Everest. Whoever was haunting Jason's house was emanating negative energy like nobody's business, and, being attuned to such things, it was hitting me like a punch from Mike Tyson in his prime. I suspected Nick was getting the same sensation. Someone *really* didn't want us up there.

I paused to let my eyes adjust to the gloom. There were no lights on upstairs, but enough light was coming from downstairs that we wouldn't walk into a table or something. There were five doors I could see, three to the left of the stairs and two on the right. One looked like a closet. Another open door I could see into enough to tell it was a bathroom. My senses were telling me the door closest, the middle bedroom, or so I assumed, was where we needed to go. I started toward it but stopped by the mirror in the hall. There were no evil faces staring back at me. Just my own, and then Nick's when he came up behind me. Robbie's finally showed as he finished mounting the stairs. His reflection actually looked more solid than he did.

"Geesh," Robbie said. "My hair's a mess."

I placed a hand on the glass, thinking I might pick up on some residual energy from the mirror. Nothing. Generally, if an object itself was haunted, I got a tingling sensation when I touched it. While I wouldn't bet the family farm on it, I was pretty sure the mirror itself wasn't the haunting force.

"Let's check out the—" I was going to say bedroom, but when the door in question creaked open on its own, I stopped and stared.

"Come into my parlor," Robbie said.

I shrugged. "He—if it is a he—knew we were coming in anyway. He's just showing off. Which is fine by me. The easier he makes this…."

Bile rose in my throat as I stepped over the threshold. The room was of average size and obviously wasn't being used. I could see piles of boxes near the center of the room, casting shadows upon the walls. The windows were curtainless, and there was enough moonlight to see. Not that there was much to see. But feel. There was a lot to feel. The hairs on my arms and the back of my neck were bristling, and I shivered involuntarily. Hopefully our nasty ghostie didn't see that. I'd hate for him to think he was getting to me.

Nick was close behind me, and I heard him say under his breath, "Holy shit."

"Yeah," I said, "he's got a lot of energy. Anger can do that. But let's see—"

I broke off when I heard Robbie cry out behind me. I spun around to find him sinking to the floor. He twisted as he fell so he landed mostly on his left side. Suddenly, he was nearly transparent, a mere wisp of a human form. I moved past Nick quickly and got down to see what was wrong.

"What the fuck?" Robbie whispered.

I tried to grab hold of his hand. There wasn't enough there to grab. "What's wrong?" I asked as I desperately tried to find some part of Robbie that was solid enough to hold. I tried to stroke the side of his face, but my hand went right through him.

"Don't know," he said weakly. He closed his eyes, and I suspected it was taking every ounce of his strength just to remain with us, even as insubstantial as he was.

A laugh, and not a nice one, came from all around us. It seemed to come out of the walls and even the ceiling and floor. A deep, guttural sound that sent chills down my spine. Only part of me was listening to it, though. I was too concerned with Robbie's condition to care much for some specter that was finding the situation humorous.

And in truth, he didn't look good. Beads of sweat were showing on his forehead—not that I could see much of his forehead, what with the dim light and the fact that he was hardly there. The sweat was a remnant of his living life, of course. Ghosts don't technically breathe, sweat, or go to the bathroom. However, something in their minds remembered what happened in certain situations, and their bodies automatically mimicked that. Even now, Robbie's chest was struggling to rise and fall with each "breath" he was taking, and a moan escaped his lips.

"I'm here," I said, for lack of anything helpful to say.

"Really?" Robbie asked, a thin smile on his lips. "I thought you'd popped out for coffee."

Nick got down on his haunches next to me, concern all over his face. Concern and, I think, a little bit of fear. The mocking laughter was still going on, and it was beginning to try my nerves. It was making Nick fidgety. "What happened to him?"

"Near as I can tell, our friendly ghost zapped all the energy out of Robbie."

"They can do that?"

"This one can, apparently."

Robbie tried a chuckle. It was marginally successful. "I feel like I got hit by a truck. Did anyone get the license plate number?" He tried to raise his head.

"Hold still," I warned him. "Gather your energy. Once you're feeling up to it, we're getting you out of here." I turned to Nick. "Look after him."

"Why? What are you—"

I rose, and as I got to my feet, the ghostly laughter ceased. I took a few steps farther into the room and addressed the air around me. "Cute. Real cute. Bet you think you're real clever, don't you?"

I wasn't expecting an answer, but I got one, of sorts. In the corner of the room, one of the shadows shifted and grew. It rose on the wall until it formed a human shape, tall and somehow malignant-looking.

"That the best you can do? Don't want to show yourself properly?"

The deep laughter returned, only now it was coming from the shadow and not the walls.

"Thing is," I said, stepping even closer to the shadow, "you may think you've scored points, but what you've really done is piss me off. And that was a really dumb thing to do."

The shadow moved, coming off the wall. Now it was a black form, a little taller than me, with broad shoulders and what looked like long, straight hair. Hard to tell when you were looking at a shadow, but it seemed to have a bushy beard. It came close to me and began to shift again. Features began to form, and in seconds, I was looking at what appeared to be a middle-aged man, his face pockmarked and not pleasant to behold. The sneer on his lips matched his eyes, which seemed to emanate hatred. He was dressed in a frock coat, and a neatly tied cravat was at his neck. Dapper, our spirit. Dapper and downright mean. Time to let him know he needed to knock it off.

"I don't know who you think you are," I said, "but I've dealt with ghosts my whole life, and you don't scare me. And you're going to regret what you just did to Robbie." To show just how unafraid I was, I took a step closer. Me and Mr. Ugly were now a little less than two feet apart. Strangely, I could smell him, something that didn't happen often with ghosts. Generally, their odor is neutral, but this sucker smelled of damp earth. Like he'd recently crawled out of his grave. I gave him my best angry glare. "Now, what do you have to say for yourself?"

He answered, but not verbally. His right hand shot out so quickly, I didn't have time to react. He grasped me by the throat and squeezed. Hard. Impossibly hard. As a ghost, he shouldn't have the strength to do that, but he felt as solid as any thug I'd ever traded slugs with.

My throat made those noises one made when your air supply was suddenly cut off. I grabbed hold of his arm and tried to shake him off, but both my hands couldn't shift him. He increased the pressure on my throat and even began to raise me up until I was barely touching the floor. My lungs fought for air, but they weren't getting any. Things were starting to go woozy, and I started feeling weaker and weaker. Vaguely, I heard Nick shouting something, and I think he had come over and was trying to dislodge the brute's hand from around my throat, but by then, I wasn't really sure about my surroundings much.

CHAPTER 4

MY BRAIN went into overdrive. If he was solid enough to manhandle me as he was doing, maybe he was solid enough to feel a blow. He was a much stronger man than I was, and I wasn't at my peak, what with the strangling and all, but there was one point in a man's anatomy that was pretty vulnerable. I raised my knee with as much force as I could muster and rammed it into his groin.

The spirit immediately vanished, and I found myself crashing to the floor. I coughed, wheezed, and then did some more coughing. Coughing and wheezing felt good. My throat felt like it had been crushed, but obviously something was now getting to the lungs. I felt hands on me, trying to help me up to a sitting position. I knew Nick was there, but it took a few minutes for my eyes to decide they wanted to see properly again.

I tried to say something, just to make sure I still could. What came out was a cough that may have been a word when it started coming out of my throat but gave up too soon. I tried again. "Had him right where I wanted him," I said. I sounded like I was doing an impersonation of Harvey Fierstein. Maybe, I wondered, the same thing had happened to Harvey years ago—being choked by a nasty ghost, I mean—and that's why his voice was the way it was.

Nick wasn't sure what he was supposed to do, so he tentatively helped me up to my feet, doing it so slowly that I felt like a maiden aunt who had fallen down. He looked at me. "You kicked a ghost in the nads."

"Seemed like the thing to do." Now I sounded more like myself. "Although, technically, I kicked *at* a ghost's nads. He vanished before I made contact."

"Still...."

"Yeah," I said. "You never see that on *Ghost Hunters*, do you?"

Robbie was stirring, so we went back over to where he was sprawled. He was up on one elbow and still barely visible, but at least he was moving. "Who is that guy?"

"Don't know," I said. "But something seems to have annoyed him." I got down next to Robbie and examined his pale face. "Are you going to be okay?"

He nodded. "By Easter, I'm hoping to feel good enough to get off this damned floor."

There was a commotion on the stairs, and soon Jason and Anthony, both of whom looked worried, joined us. "Is everyone okay?" Jason asked.

"We heard one hell of a crash," Anthony added.

I got to my feet. "Just introducing ourselves to your ghost. I must say he's not the nicest guy I've ever met, dead or alive."

Nick indicated the spot where the spirit had manifested. "The ghost came off the wall over there and grabbed Duncan by the throat and nearly throttled him to death."

The couple's faces both lost their color until they were nearly as pale as Robbie. I grimaced at Nick. "Thanks for not alarming them."

Anthony was obviously worried, but part of him was still skeptical. "You saw a ghost?"

"Saw and felt. He was very solid, at least when he was choking me."

Jason took a further step into the room, which meant he was now standing on Robbie. Well, his right foot was going right through Robbie's side. "It *does* feel like something odd's here in the room. There's a weird kind of chill. It's going right through me!"

"That's because," I said, "you're standing on your cousin's ghost. Robbie's lying right there on the floor. Your foot's sticking through him."

I admit it may have been a bit much to take in all at once. Shocked, Jason jerked his leg away and lost his balance. He would have toppled over if Anthony hadn't been there to steady him. "What?" he said, his eyes not leaving the floor. "What? My cousin? Robbie?"

Robbie must have soaked in some of Jason's energy, because now there was even a little color in his face. He glared at me. "Speaking of not being alarming."

I shrugged. "I figured you weren't going to be well enough to leave for several hours at least, and I couldn't have people just walking through you all night."

Anthony was confused. "Wait. What? You're saying there's a ghost right there?"

"Cuter and friendlier than Casper," I said as Robbie wiggled his fingers at the couple, who had now backed up to the doorway. "Jason, your cousin says hi."

I've always read that people don't faint unless there's some sort of medical condition. One didn't, supposedly, faint from shock. Jason looked like he was going to test that theory, and I think that if Anthony weren't still holding him from his near-backward tumble, he'd have joined Robbie on the floor. "I need a drink," he muttered.

"SO HE'S sitting right there," Jason said, indicating the "empty" chair at the kitchen table, where we had congregated for explanations and alcohol.

"Looking right at you," I replied.

"Why can't I see him?"

I made a "who knows?" gesture with my hands. "Most people can't. Some can see ghosts a little. They show up as shadows or mists. A few, like myself and Nick here, can see them clearly."

Robbie was slumped over the table, holding his head in his hands. If I didn't know better, I'd say he had the flu. He looked weak and feverish, and his hair appeared damp and was sticking out from him running his hands through it. He groaned. "I feel like shit. Stinky shit. Shit that other shit doesn't even want to be around."

"And," I added, "hear them plainly too. Sometimes unfortunately."

Anthony shook his head. He was nursing a large gin and tonic and mainly seemed interested in clutching the cold glass tightly. He looked at his lover. "I don't understand. Didn't you tell me your cousin Robbie died over ten years ago?"

Jason looked uncertain. "He did."

"Dying was easy," Robbie said with a moan. "This shit is hard."

It was one of those times when I really wished I could touch him. Just lay a hand on his shoulder to let him know I was there and that I cared. I placed a hand on the arm of his chair instead. Best I could do. "You're looking better."

He was rubbing his eyes and paused to let one heavy-lidded eye gaze at me. "Really? What the hell did I look like before?"

Jason asked Nick, "And you can see him?

Nick nodded. He had opted for mere soda, but every now and then I caught him eying Anthony's nearly untouched gin with envy. He picked up his own glass and put it to his lips and then realized there was nothing but ice left. He set the glass back down and looked miserable. The mood around the table, it must be said, wasn't festive.

"But I could see the face in the mirror," Jason said. "That was a ghost, wasn't it? I saw it. Why can I see that face, but I can't see Robbie?"

"It doesn't take much energy for spirits to show in reflective surfaces," I explained. "They can appear in mirrors and such fairly easily and with enough oomph that even people with almost no psy abilities can see them. You obviously have more than Anthony, who's never seen the face." Anthony looked almost affronted, so I amended. "I'm just guessing." Gee, intimate that people have no psychic powers, and they get all huffy.

Nick broke into the conversation, asking Jason, "What did your uncle look like?"

The question threw the guy off guard, and he had to think a moment. "Thin. He wasn't real tall. Kind of ordinary, I guess."

"No beard?"

Jason shook his head.

"Then our ghost isn't your uncle," Nick stated. "So he must have been a previous resident. Do you know who owned the house before your aunt and uncle?"

Again, a head shake.

"I can check out the library tomorrow morning," Nick said to me. "See if we can find out who we're dealing with. Check out the old property maps."

Anthony said, "I think the house was built around 1890. A lot of houses on this block date from that period."

I had finished my drink almost as soon as it had been handed to me, also a gin and tonic. It had felt soothing going down my throat, but maybe it hadn't been such a great idea to ingest that much alcohol so quickly. My head was feeling the effects. Not that I was tipsy, mind you. Just saying I could feel the booze inside me. Another drink would be wonderful, but it was getting late, and we'd have to be heading out soon. I forced myself to think about the situation at hand and not potent potables. "Obviously, our friend the ghost isn't going to leave of his own free will."

"He didn't seem a reasonable type of guy," Nick agreed.

"He was probably insane when he died. That makes for a very powerful spirit. And if he died violently, that gives him even more mojo."

"Ghosts have mojo?" Anthony asked, bemused.

"This one used to have mojo," Robbie moaned. "It got stomped out of me."

"For want of a better word," I told Anthony. "Energy, mojo. Whatever gives them the power to interact with the living world. And since our friend upstairs won't leave on his own, we'll have to force him. If we find out his name and something about his life, that makes things easier. We can research tomorrow and come back tomorrow night and finish things up, if that works for you guys."

They agreed. Jason continued to steal glances at where Robbie was sitting. "It's so weird to think he's been around all this time. Why hasn't he come to visit?"

Robbie was too busy feeling horrible to supply an answer I could then tell his cousin, so I said, "He may have. But you wouldn't have known he was there. I know he visits his parents every now and then, but not often and not for long. He finds it hard to be around them and know that they can't see him."

"Yeah," Robbie muttered, "what you said."

"Can you tell him," Jason asked, "that I felt really bad about what happened to him? His life cut short like that? I mean, our families were never really that close, but I always liked him. We played together sometimes when we were kids."

"And he fucking cheated when we played Monopoly. Worst banker ever." Robbie laid his head on the table. "Someone kill me."

"You're already dead," I told him. In truth, I was more than a little worried about him. I'd often seen him zapped of energy, but it had never been like this. This was more like he was physically ill, which, considering he didn't really have a body, was impossible.

"Gee," he said as he raised his head back up, "I'd forgotten. And here I thought all that walking through walls stuff was just me being all Criss Angel." He attempted to sit straight, but he just wasn't feeling up to it. Robbie slumped against the chair back, looking defeated.

"We'd better get you home, if you feel well enough to travel. You can rest better there, away from energy-sucking spirits."

Jason's head swiveled from me to what was, for him, an empty chair, and back to me. "It's weird when you're talking to him. It's like hearing one part of a telephone conversation."

"I think I can get myself out to the car," Robbie said. "I like cars. Cars get me far away from this place. Let's go to the car."

As I rose, I asked Jason and Anthony, "You guys have somewhere you can stay tonight?"

Anthony blinked. "Is that necessary? I mean, we've been here for several weeks now, and we haven't been attacked or anything. Just noises and things moving and—"

"He knows we're after him now," I said. "And we've put him in a really pissy mood. I wouldn't stay here, if I were you."

Jason sighed heavily. "We can stay at my mom's. Tell her we were painting or something, and the fumes were too overpowering for us to sleep."

"Oh, hey," Robbie said, "tell Aunt Nancy I said hi." He was beginning to sound more like his old self. Maybe it was just the idea of getting out of the house, but he even seemed to have more color to him.

"I think it would be best," I said to Jason. "We'll call you tomorrow when we're ready to come out, and with any luck, we'll zap this ghost quickly, and you two can have your house back."

Jason nodded. "Sounds good."

It did. I had the feeling, though, that I was being too hopeful. Something was wrong here. No usual ghost should be able to do to Robbie what this guy had. I didn't want to alarm Jason and Anthony, but they had inherited not only a house but a megapowerful ghost along with it. One, I felt in my bones, who wasn't going to be easy to get rid of.

CHAPTER 5

THE APARTMENT felt strangely empty. Robbie was there. I could feel him like a presence that was just out of my mental sight, but he was in the ghost equivalent of sleep. Daisy was sleeping as well, snoring away in her corner of the bedroom, tuckered out from a particularly strenuous afternoon of chasing squirrels. Every now and then, she'd rouse herself just enough to raise her head and see if anything was going on she should know about. Satisfied, she'd lower her head back onto the pillow of her doggie bed, and soon she'd be sawing logs again.

I spent most of my time playing Solitaire on the computer. Earlier, I'd been at the library with Nick, but I'd grown restless when our research didn't come up with much. Nick finally had enough with my grumbling and pacing and said he'd rather continue on his own. Leaving the library, I'd realized I was still worried about Robbie, and that feeling hadn't changed when I got home and found that he still didn't have the energy to appear.

I was putting a black jack on a red queen when a sudden snort came to my ears. For half a second, I thought it was Robbie making a welcome appearance, but then I realized it was Daisy. I looked over at her. The snort hadn't wakened her, but she shifted in her sleep and even licked her lips. There was a tiny bit of squirrel blood on her jowls that she slurped off. I guess I'd missed a bit when I'd wiped her face after we'd left the park.

"I wonder what you dream about," I said softly. The dog's chest was rising and falling, even though she didn't need to breathe. Habit, I guess. She didn't answer. I turned back to my game. There was a red

Stephen Osborne

ten I hadn't realized was hanging around, waiting to go on that black jack. I electronically flipped cards over until I had no moves left. The trouble with computer Solitaire was that it didn't allow you to cheat. I mean, come on. If you couldn't cheat when playing Solitaire, what was the point? I turned off the computer.

I sat for a moment, listening to Daisy and wondering if Nick was having any better luck than we'd had earlier and if Robbie was anywhere close to recovered when my cell phone chirped. The noise sounded extremely loud after all the quiet, and I fumbled to get the phone out of my pocket to answer before it rang again, not wanting to disturb Robbie any more than necessary. Finally, I got it out.

"Hello?" I asked.

"Is this Duncan Andrews?"

The voice was gruff, and something about the tone made the hairs on the back of my neck stand up. "If it isn't, my dear old Granny has been lying to me all these years."

The joke didn't get a laugh, not that I expected it to. The speaker merely grunted and then said, "How much do you know about Mark Callahan?"

The name almost didn't register for a second, as I always thought of Gina's boyfriend as Mark the Dentist. His last name came up so rarely that I nearly said, "Who?" Instead I asked, "Who is this?"

"A friend," Gruff Voice said. He added, "Not that you'd think so, but I am. I've got information for you."

"I bet you do," I said. The conversation woke Daisy up. She sat up in her bed, gazing at me with her bloodshot eyes. Maybe, like me, she could sense the person speaking with me on the phone wasn't a person at all, but some kind of supernatural creature. I assumed it was a demon. It had that throaty voice so common to demons. "So what do you think you know about Mark?"

The caller laughed, if you could call a series of strident barks laughing. "Not so fast, Mr. Andrews. My information isn't free."

"Of course it isn't."

"Can you meet me tonight? At ten o'clock?"

52

At ten, I hoped we'd be leaving Jason Church's house, having vanquished yet another nasty spirit. "No can do. If you want to meet, it will have to be earlier. Say, like, now."

That threw the caller a little. He sputtered. "I… I don't think I can do that. Later. We must make it later."

"Because you're a demon, and you don't like to slink out until after the sun goes down?" My question wasn't met with a denial, so I assumed I'd hit the mark. "I'll come to you. Just tell me you're not one of those sewer dwellers. Because, honestly, that would be a deal breaker right there."

"I'm at a warehouse. On Massachusetts. Near Theatre on the Square."

He gave me the address, which I jotted down on a notepad. A question popped into my head, and I just had to ask it. "You have a cell phone?"

"Got it off some guy last night. He was delicious."

Sorry I asked. "I'll be there."

"I want money," the demon growled. "Five thousand dollars."

"Yeah, I'll stop by an ATM on the way," I replied, letting the sarcasm drip.

"The information isn't free, Andrews."

"And whatever it is, I'm sure it's not worth five thou. I'll bring five hundred, and you'll just have to settle."

Haggling with a demon wasn't easy, because once they had their mind on something, they hated to give it up, but I finally convinced my scratchy-voiced friend the sum he was asking was out of the question. I actually had no intention of giving him any money at all, as I didn't believe he had anything of interest for me. Plus he was a demon. But I was interested in finding out how he knew I was familiar with Mark the Dentist. Demons weren't exactly social creatures and rarely hung out at cocktail parties, so I didn't think he'd learned of the connection through casual conversation. Plus, what the heck was a demon doing with my phone number? Wasn't that a bit like the Frankenstein monster having the torch-wielding villagers on speed dial, just in case he got bored one night?

I first called Nick to tell him I'd be slightly delayed, and then I called Jason and told him the same thing. Before leaving the apartment, I made sure Daisy was comfortably settled and had water—which, again, she didn't technically need but drank anyway—and put on my shoulder holster. The .38 felt nice at my side, but not as nice as the silver dagger I put in a sheath around my right arm. Bullets annoyed the hell out of demons, but didn't do any real damage. Silver, however, would kill them.

I paused at the door and reached out with my senses. Robbie still wasn't up and around, although now I had more of a feel that he was there, resting and gathering energy. "Rest well," I told the air before heading out.

The warehouse the demon was in was one I'd passed many times. Although the area had been redeveloped and was now a young professionals heaven, with coffee shops, live theater, and several bars to help them spend their money, the one spot that seemed to have been overlooked was this warehouse, an eyesore that looked like it might fall down before someone decided to tear it down. I found a vacant spot to park along Massachusetts Avenue and walked the half block to the place.

The windows had been blacked out, and several panes had been broken and were boarded over. Not an enticing edifice. One side of the brick building had once had an advertisement painted onto it, but now the artwork was so faded it would have been hard to tell what product was being touted, even if there had been sufficient light to see it. The building seemed to be all imposing shadows, as if even the streetlights were afraid to illuminate the place.

I went to a side door. Paint was peeling off the woodwork, and it looked like one good kick would get me inside, but when I tried the doorknob, I found it was unlocked. I went in, getting a flashlight out of my jacket pocket as I crossed the threshold. I switched it on and shut the door behind me.

The beam of light didn't show me much. Dusty floor, big, bare room, dirty walls with loads of graffiti scrawls, and a few boxes and trash scattered around. There was little or no light coming in from the windows that weren't boarded up, so my flashlight was all I had to see by. Just for giggles, I found a light switch and tried it. Nothing. I scanned the room again. From what I could see, there was the main room that I was in. There were some stairs off to my right, and at the far end of the room were some doors that must have led to offices when the warehouse had been a working concern. No demons in sight, but my senses were telling me something nasty wasn't far off.

I figured it wouldn't hurt to be cautious, so I pulled out my gun, holding it in my left hand while the flashlight stayed in my right. I crept farther into the room, my feet crunching on some broken glass at one point. Something scuttled off to my left. A rat, no doubt. You'd think a rat would be smart enough not to stick around in a warehouse that held a demon, but maybe it wasn't one of your more brilliant rats. I got to the far end and tried one of the office doors. It creaked open, and I saw a small room that still had an old wooden desk in it. No chair, and not much else. The legs of the desk were covered with cobwebs.

The other offices were similarly barren. Conspicuous by its absence was a demon. Surely he'd heard me by now, shuffling around. I left the office area and went to the stairs. A quick tour up there revealed lots of rooms and lots of junk and cobwebs, and even an old ten-speed bicycle with no wheels, but no demon. I returned back to the main floor and was about to give up and leave when my flashlight revealed another set of stairs on the other side of the room, leading down.

Great. A creepy basement. Just what I needed to make my day complete.

There was no handrail, and the steps weren't in the best condition. If the demon didn't kill me, I'd complain to OSHA. Every step I took down, the rotted wood creaked loudly, announcing my presence. When I reached the bottom step, I heard the scratch of a match, and suddenly there was light in the dingy room.

I stopped, one foot on the floor and one still on the last step, staring at the now-illuminated figure in the center of the room. Some demons— and demons came in more varieties than Heinz—were big and scaly and some weird color like bright green or chartreuse and couldn't blend in with society if they tried. Some, like the one who had just lit an oil lamp so we'd have some light, were close to human looking. This one wore a dingy suit that could have come from Goodwill but more likely had belonged to some poor schmuck the demon had killed. He was yellowish in hue and had a nearly human face. In fact, he sort of resembled Elton John, if Elton John were jaundiced and had a ridged forehead and large, pointed teeth he couldn't quite close his lips around. The demon even wore black-framed glasses and had either brown hair in a Beatles cut or a toupee. There were two horns sticking up out of his head that sort of ruined the whole Elton vibe.

Elton the Demon was sitting at a wooden desk that had seen better days. It was missing a leg, making the rusty oil lamp on it lean at a dangerous angle, looking like it might slide off at any moment. Elton had been smoking. There were several butts in a battered ashtray, and one had smoke coiling up from it, having been freshly ground out.

"You took your time," the demon growled.

I clicked off the flashlight and stowed it away in my jacket pocket. "Traffic was a bitch," I said, pointing the gun at him.

Elton didn't flinch. There was no reason for him to, as he knew a bullet would only be a minor irritation. "Bring the money?"

I shook my head. "I've got Eddie from Bank of America out in my car, though, with a briefcase full of cash. I give the word, and he comes in, and you can bathe in greenbacks."

The ridged forehead furrowed. "Funny. I want money, Andrews. The information I have is worth it."

"What do you want money for? To buy a better toupee?"

The demon scooted his rickety chair back and stood. Goodness, he was tall. He had little piggy eyes he was aiming at me angrily, but little piggy eyes with nearly seven feet of muscular demon attached to them have some power. "If you don't want my info…." He shrugged.

I stashed the .38 back into the holster and walked over to the desk. As I walked, I took in the room, or what I could see of it. The demon had made quite a nice little hovel of the place. There was a bed over to one side and a bookshelf nearby, crammed with paperbacks. I fought the urge to go over and check out the titles. I mean, who wouldn't want to know the reading tastes of a demon who vaguely resembled Elton John? I leaned against the desk, trying to look casual, which isn't easy when a big yellow guy is towering over you with a little bit of drool escaping from his mottled red lips.

"Don't get your junk into a twist," I told the big guy. "If—and that's a big if—your info turns out to be legit, I'll see that you're compensated. I didn't bring the cash with me because, well, to be truthful, I don't think you've got anything worth paying for. That, and I figured you'd just kill me and steal the cash."

The demon pondered these words and then nodded in agreement. "Cautious. I can understand that."

I met his beady little eyes. "I do have a couple of points I'd like to make. First, if you're bluffing and have nothing, I'll kill you."

He didn't look too worried, as if better humans than me had threatened him. "I'm not," he said simply.

"And if you do have the goods and get my money, I want you to leave town."

Elton the Demon scoffed. "Like I want to stick around here."

"Okay." I favored him with a smile. "Dazzle me."

He sat back down and pulled a pack of cigarettes out of his breast pocket. He stuck one between his lips and used a neon-blue Bic lighter that had been lying on the desk to light it. He took a long drag, exhaled, and then said, "How much do you know about Mark Callahan?"

"I know he's a dentist. He's lived here for a few years. Not much else."

"What do you know about the Order of Cotton Mather?"

I shook my head. "Never heard of them."

Elton shrugged. "I'm not surprised. There're not many of them around nowadays. They're a fanatical sect, bent on destroying the last witches on Earth."

"And you're suggesting that Mark is a member of this order?"

"Right the first time, Andrews."

Part of me wanted to stab the life right out of Elton and walk away. But there was a worrying gnaw in my guts that wanted to hear more. "You've got proof of this, I'm sure."

Elton pulled open the top desk drawer and extracted a manila envelope. He tossed it over to me.

Inside, I found photographs, newspaper clippings, and items printed off the Internet. I sifted through the lot quickly at first, but what I saw on even a cursory look chilled my blood. I went back to a few of the photos. One was old, a black-and-white snapshot of several men standing around a tree. Most of the men had their backs to the camera, but one face could be seen in profile. It was Mark Callahan. Hanging from the tree by a noose was a young woman.

The other pictures weren't any nicer. In one, a young man was tied to a chair. He was battered and bloody and looked like he'd been tortured to the brink of death. This picture was in color, but there was a slight blur, making it hard to see who the men standing around the chair were. One looked very much like Mark. I looked carefully. Too much like him.

There was an article, clipped from a cheap magazine, all about the Order of Cotton Mather. An unidentified member of the cult had been interviewed. I scanned the pages quickly, but one quote stuck out. "They're all over," the cult member said. "They look like you or me, but they're not. They're creatures of unimaginable power. They're dangerous. They can live for centuries, taking on different forms. They must be hunted down and destroyed. That's our job."

Another sheet was something copied from an Internet blog. There was no indication who the author was or when the item had been posted. I didn't bother to read all of it, but the ending paragraph caught my eye. "We have recently learned there are at least two in Indiana. One in South Bend, the other in Indianapolis. My partner and I will investigate, and if what we've been told is true, we will summon other members to deal with the situation."

I don't know how long I stood gazing at the documents Elton had given me. I was vaguely aware he'd started on another cigarette while he waited. Finally, I looked up. "Where did you get these?"

"Does it matter?" he replied, blowing out smoke.

I shook my head. I flipped through the photographs again. Several showed people either being hanged or the aftermath, a bloated corpse dangling from a tree. One was of a person, hard to tell if it was male or female, being burned at the stake. "Why show them to me?" I asked. Demons weren't known for doing good deeds, even for money.

Elton leaned back in his chair, which creaked like it was about to collapse right out from under him. "I have an old score to settle with the Order of Cotton Mather. While they primarily target witches, they aren't exactly pals with my kind either. Plus I'm in need of cash. I want to travel a bit." Here he waved his cigarette, indicating his squalid quarters. "Get away from this. I heard, through the underground, that you were friends with a witch. I did some checking and learned that Mark Callahan was dating a friend of yours. Put two and two together."

For a demon, Elton was being pretty reasonable. Most I'd met, even if they had contacted me to exchange information for money, couldn't have overridden their desire to kill long enough to sit down and discuss business. Elton seemed to be striving to be at least somewhat human. The suit, the smoking, and the case full of books.

He set his cigarette in a butt-filled ashtray. I watched the smoke curling up. "Those things will kill you," I said. He gave me an exasperated look. I put the articles and photos back into the envelope. "I'll have to check these out, make sure they're authentic—"

"They are."

"If they are, I'll come back with some money for you. Not sure how far it will get you, but I'll see what I can do."

He looked like he was going to argue but then nodded. "Don't take too long."

"I won't." Which was the truth. If Mark really was involved with some witch-hunting organization, I wasn't going to tarry. And my gut feeling was, despite where the information had come from, it was legit.

"YOU'RE AWFULLY quiet."

I was so deep in thought that I'd nearly forgotten Nick was in the car with me. We were heading to the Victorian house on Denmark

Street, but in truth, my mind wasn't on my driving. I was thinking about Mark the Dentist, who might be Mark the Witch Hunter, and I wasn't coming to any conclusions. Surely if Mark was what Elton claimed, Gina would be toast by now. After all, she had come out and admitted to Mark she was a witch. Why hadn't he acted? It didn't make sense. But then, neither did Elton's info. It struck me as legit. It *had* been Mark in those photos, and I didn't think any photoshopping had been used to tinker with the images.

Nick's statement broke me out of my reverie. "Just thinking," I told him. I thought about telling him of my meeting with Elton, but something held me back. Maybe by telling Nick about my concerns of Mark the Dentist, I would make them more real somehow. I decided I'd tell him later, after we zapped the evil entity haunting Jason Church and his family.

I decided to change the subject. "Have you found out anything else about the history of the house?"

Nick smiled weakly. "Unfortunately, yes. I think I know who our ghost is."

"You don't sound enthused."

"If it's who I think, he's one hell of a nasty character. You may have heard of him. Dr. Stanley Moore."

The name did seem familiar, and I racked my brain trying to recall where I'd heard it. Finally, it came to me. "The serial killer?"

"The same. The reason we were having trouble finding out anything about the house before 1940 was because of a change in the postal code. The house numbers in that area were all changed. But, as far as I can tell, Dr. Moore owned that house from 1923 to 1938, and it was there that he murdered all those boys."

The details of Moore's crimes were coming back to me. He had lured young men to his house, often mere teenagers, with offers of a free place to live. Most of his victims had been street kids with no home of their own or, in some cases, a home life so poor and so devoid of hope that the prospect of moving into a large house in the fashionable district of downtown Indianapolis was too great. Moore would make the boys his sexual toys for a few weeks and lavish them with gifts and promises. Unfortunately, something always set the good doctor off, and he ended up killing each and every one of them, burying them all in the basement.

"Didn't Moore kill himself?" I asked.

Nick nodded. "He was found next to the corpse of his seventh victim." Nick had been holding a notebook, which he now opened to consult his notes. "One Benjamin Tumbridge. Tumbridge was seventeen when Dr. Moore took him in and from all accounts had lived the longest with Moore. They were about to celebrate one year together when something snapped in the doctor, and he hacked up Tumbridge with a butcher knife. Moore then shot himself in the chest with his old service revolver. It wasn't until days later that the bodies were found. Strangely, Moore's head was missing when they discovered the bodies. Someone had come along after the fact and decapitated him. The head was never found."

"Fun. So we're dealing with one fucked-up spirit. Insane and a murderer."

"Seems so." Nick closed his notebook. "What I can't figure out, though, is why he's rearing his ugly head now. I mean, if he died in 1938, why wait until now to start haunting the place?"

"Maybe," I said, "he's always been there but simply biding his time. After all, the house was owned for ages by Jason's aunt and uncle. And when the uncle died, there was just Auntie living there for decades. Not much to excite a predatory fuck like Dr. Moore. And then Jason and his boyfriend move in. A gay couple, and they have a young son. Probably younger than Moore liked them, but he was an insane asshole; who knows what goes on in his mind. They may have stirred some passions in the dormant spirit."

"You're probably right," Nick said.

He glanced out of the window. We were approaching 175 Denmark. All the lights were off in the house, and it loomed like a black shadow. There were cheering lights on in the houses on either side, making the dark edifice even creepier in comparison. There was a lone figure on the sidewalk in front of the house, and as we got closer, I could see it was Jason Church, bundled in a heavy coat and a fur-lined hat. He was holding his arms close to his body, and his face lit up when I pulled up to the curb to park. I hoped he hadn't been waiting long. The temperature had fallen, and the weather pundits were calling for the first snow of the season. Getting out of the car, I watched my breath coming out in white puffs and thought for once they were probably correct in their predictions. It felt like snow was coming. Nick and I joined Jason on the sidewalk.

"I did like you said. I didn't go inside."

"Yeah," I said. "Probably not safe. We think we know whom we're dealing with. Your ghost is one Dr. Stanley Moore."

The name obviously meant nothing to Jason, so Nick filled him in. "He was the city's most infamous serial killer. Killed seven young men before killing himself in 1938."

Jason's eyes bulged. "My aunt lived in a murder house all those years?"

I clapped a hand on his shoulder. "Yeah, I'm guessing the real estate people didn't fill her in on that little detail. But now we know who we're dealing with, which makes our job easier." I looked around, seeing what must be Jason's car in the driveway but not much else. There was no one on the street, and even the traffic coming down Denmark was sparse. Most people, it seemed, had chosen to stay in their nice warm abodes rather than come out on such a chilly night. "Anthony didn't come with you?"

Jason shook his head. "He opted to stay with Gary at Anthony's mom's tonight."

Wise, I thought. If I had been Anthony, wild horses couldn't have dragged me back to a house where strange faces showed up in mirrors. "You don't have to come in if you don't want to. In fact, I'm sure it's safer out here. You can stay in your car until we're done."

"I'll go in." Jason's voice was shaky, and who could blame him?

Nick and I went around my car to the trunk, which I opened so we could get out the two shotguns I had stowed there. There were double-barreled Winchesters loaded with rock salt. I handed one to Nick. He stared at it as if I'd just put a boa constrictor in his mitts.

"I've never used one of these," he said. He was holding the shotgun away from his body as if it were hot and might singe his clothes if it got too close.

"They're easy to use," I said. "Point the end with the holes at the nasty thing that you want to shoot. You'll see there are two triggers. Pull back on one of them. Nasty thing will go away."

"That will kill it?"

"Nope, but the salt disperses the energy. Don't ask me how, but it does. Nasty thing has to go away and regroup."

"Do you think," Nick asked, "that there's any chance we can reason with this guy?" He didn't sound hopeful.

I shook my head. "I'll tell you what's going to go down. We have to confront this bastard. Let him know that we know who he is. Then we exorcize his ass, banish him to wherever. Then Jason and Anthony get their house back, and we can go home and know that we've done good."

"Have you done many exorcisms?"

"A fair few." In actuality, that was more Gina's department. Usually, when we dealt with evil spirits, I kept them busy while she made with the magic words. And part of me wanted to call her so she could be handy, but I knew I couldn't face her after my little chat with Elton. My face would give me away, and she'd want to know why I was bothered. No, before I saw Gina, I would have to do some checking on my own to make sure Elton wasn't feeding me a lot of hogwash, and then I'd have to have words with a certain dentist. "Technically, what we're doing is a banishment. An exorcism is for when someone is possessed by a nasty."

"Oh." Nick nodded. "And how does a banishment work? Is there a specific text you read, or—"

"Usually I just cuss at the spirit a lot and tell him to get the fuck out."

"And that works, does it?"

I shrugged. "Mostly."

Nick's eyebrows shot up. "Mostly? We're going in to confront a mean-assed, murdering jerkface ghost, and the best you can give me is *mostly*?"

I grabbed a small bag out of the trunk. "Sorry. Should I have lied?"

"Yes!"

I closed the trunk. "We'll knock old Doc Moore into oblivion."

"That's better."

We rejoined Jason, who, by his furtive looks at the house and the shuffling of his feet, was growing more nervous by the minute. I handed him the small bag. "What's in this?" he asked.

"The proverbial bell, book, and candle." I was going to have Nick use those items while I ventured inside the house by myself, but if Jason insisted on helping, he could do the task. "When we go inside, you stay on the porch. Once we cross the threshold, you ring the bell. Then you light the candle and start reading from the Bible. I've marked some passages. Psalms. You read those aloud, over and over. If the candle blows out on its own, you'll know we've been successful, and you can stop reading. When we come back out, you ring the bell again, signifying the end of the ritual."

"So I stay outside?" Jason didn't sound too upset by the idea.

"Someone has to."

He nodded as he opened up the bag. "Okay, tell me again what I've got to do. I don't want to mess it up."

I went over his task again and even opened up the Bible to the relevant passages. As I did so, I had my back to the front door, but even without seeing the entryway, I could feel a change coming over the house. In my mind, I could see a blackness forming. Deep shadows were engulfing the rooms, infesting the floors and the walls. It was as if Dr. Moore's evil was seeping into the very woodwork. Nick stood behind Jason, trying to look helpful. I wondered if he could sense the blackness forming within 175 Denmark Street.

Finally, Jason felt confident he knew what to do, and Nick and I prepared to enter. Jason got down on his haunches and began to get the candle ready, a stubby white one I'd gotten from Gina's storeroom. I glanced at Nick. "Ready?" I asked.

He glared at me. "You're kidding, right?"

"Thought I'd ask." I grasped the doorknob, half-expecting the damn thing to burst into flames on contact. I also thought the door might not even open, an old trick sneaky spooks liked to pull, but it creaked open slowly, sounding like Dracula getting out of his coffin in the old movies.

The sound did little to help Nick's trepidation. "Like that's not ominous at all."

"You don't have to come with me," I said. "I can do this alone. I have, on many occasions."

Nick shook his head. "No. I need to do this."

I stepped in first and almost leaped out of my skin when there was a jarring sound directly behind us. I'd forgotten I'd told Jason to ring the bell. He looked sheepish when I jumped. "That's right, isn't it? You said as you crossed the threshold."

"Yeah," I replied.

I was just inside the doorway and felt with my hand for the light switch. After several flicks, I realized the lights weren't going to come on. Another trick, but an effective one. Navigating a somewhat unfamiliar house in near darkness wasn't easy. I reached into my jacket pocket and pulled out two small flashlights and handed one to Nick. Just for giggles, I tried the lights again. Nothing.

I turned to Jason, who was now sitting cross-legged with the lit candle and bell before him on the porch. He was holding the Bible. "Well, I can't turn on the porch light. Do the best you can reading by the light of the candle. If that doesn't work, just recite the Lord's Prayer or the Twenty-Third Psalm over and over."

Jason nodded. "Gotcha."

I motioned for Nick to step farther inside so I could close the door. Once it was shut and we were plunged into darkness, I flicked the switch on my flashlight. A nice, bright beam illuminated the foyer. Nick turned his on, but as soon as he did, mine began to dim. By the time mine went out entirely, his batteries began to give up as well.

"What's up with the flashlights?" Nick asked, his voice shaking ever so slightly.

"The good doctor doesn't want us to be able to see what we're doing. He's drained the batteries. Easy to do, for him."

Nick glanced back at the closed door. My eyes were adjusting to the darkness enough that I could see his basic movements. "What about Jason? What if he can't read those passages?"

"That's just window dressing, to give him something to do and keep him out of the house. It's not all that essential." And that was true. In similar situations, Gina had sometimes stayed out of the house in question and did the bell, book, and candle thing. Sometimes she hadn't. We still hadn't figured out if it helped or not.

"Come on," I said, slowly making my way over to the stairs, or in this case the dark area where I knew the stairs were. There was a little light coming in from the windows, but not much. Enough to keep Nick and me from tripping over an ottoman or something, but not much else. I fought the urge to stick my hands out in front of me to avoid hitting something. I wasn't going to let Doc Moore see his parlor tricks were effective.

I was aware Nick was close behind me—very close—as I got to the bottom of the steps. As I grabbed hold of the balustrade, Nick said, "Do you hear that?"

It would have been hard to miss. It sounded like every floorboard in the house was creaking. There were sounds all around us, moans and groans of wood that made it seem like we were on an old ship that was being tossed in a tempestuous sea. "He's just trying to scare us," I said.

"He shouldn't try so hard," Nick replied.

CHAPTER 6

AS WE climbed the stairs, another sound assailed our ears. Now a whistling wind had joined the cacophony, and the chandelier above the front room must have been set in motion, as the shadows it cast washed up and down on the walls around us. I was reminded of that scene in *The Exorcist* where Max Von Sydow and that other dude mount the stairs to confront the possessed Linda Blair. I just hoped we wouldn't get pea soup in our faces when we got upstairs. Of course, Max Von Sydow hadn't been toting a shotgun. Probably should have been, but hey.

Maybe it was because we were moving slowly. Maybe it was because it was so damn dark, but it seemed it was one of the longest staircases I'd ever climbed. Finally, we got to the top. The atmosphere was thick and the temperature even colder than it had been downstairs. I shivered as I pulled out a pack of matches and lit one so I could get my bearings. There was even less light upstairs, as most of the doors were closed, so our only illumination came from a tiny window at the end of the hall, and it wasn't doing such a bang-up job.

I blinked at the sudden light, even though I knew it was coming. I saw Nick's face. He looked pale, and I didn't think it was all due to being lit by a tiny flame. We were standing near the hall mirror, and Nick gasped as he saw it.

I could see the flame in my hands reflected and could see Nick and me reflected, sort of, but what really caught my eye was the fact that the mirror seemed to be dripping blood. Small rivulets of red were flowing down from the top of the mirror and streaking the glass and pooling down to the bottom frame.

"Is that blood?" Nick asked. "How can that be blood? Where's it coming from? Whose blood is it?"

I'd seen the old bleeding-mirror trick before, and bleeding walls, and once even a bleeding Westinghouse refrigerator. "I've never had it analyzed," I said, "but my guess is that it isn't blood. Not really. Just some form of ectoplasm that resembles blood."

Nick didn't look convinced by my explanation. "Could have fooled me."

I patted him on the shoulder. "Come on. Let's get this over with." I moved toward the middle bedroom and had almost reached the door when I realized Nick wasn't following. "Coming?"

"Can't you feel it?" he said. He nodded toward the door. "Evil. That's the only way to describe it. Pure evil, and it's right in there, waiting for us."

I knew exactly what Nick was experiencing. I was getting it as well—wave after wave hitting me, telling my brain to get the hell out of there. Run. Run fast. If I dared to open that door, I probably wouldn't survive. I'd felt negative energy when dealing with spirits before, but never on this scale. "I can do this on my own," I said. "You can stay out here. I'll handle old Doc Moore."

Nick snorted. "Yeah, and leave me out here by myself. No, thanks."

"He's just worried, that's why he's trying to keep us away. Using every trick at his disposal."

Squaring his shoulders, Nick said, "Well, let's show him we've got a trick or two of our own."

I went to twist the knob, but before my fingers made contact, the door slowly creaked open on its own.

Walking into the room was like wading into a pool. My legs seemed to be coming up against some force that didn't want them to go farther. The room itself was black—pitch-black. My match had gone out minutes before, so I lit another. It's not the easiest thing to light a match while cradling a shotgun under your arm. Try it sometime. Not that it helped much. Dark, ominous shapes seemed to spring up on the walls, oozing across the floor toward us. There was a low whistling sound that seemed to be coming from near the center of the room that reminded me of the sound created when you put a seashell up to your ear.

Nick was dogging my footsteps and nearly collided with me when I paused a few feet beyond the door. "Sorry," he whispered.

"You don't have to whisper," I told him.

"Says you. The doctor doesn't seem to be in a good mood, and I'm not going to be the one to piss him off."

"Let's get this over with." I took a step farther into the room, even though my legs liked being back close to the doorway. "Doctor Moore!" I shouted at the ceiling. "Yeah, that's right! We know who you are! So let's stop playing games, and you come on out to face us."

The air around us suddenly became chilled, and I had to force myself not to shiver. There also was the return of the phantom wind, which seemed to swirl around the bedroom. My hair wasn't really long enough to be ruffled by the gust, but Nick's do was immediately messed up. My pitiful little match went out, but a sideways glance showed me that Nick had to squint with the wind hitting his face. So did I.

Nick reached out and grabbed the back of my jacket, probably to anchor himself to something in the pitch-blackness we found ourselves in. "I can't see shit, Duncan!" Nick had to shout over the otherworldly wind.

"Neither can I," I admitted. "But luckily, I have some tricks of my own!" I cradled the shotgun under my armpit so I could get a small ball out of my pocket, a plastic little bauble I'd grabbed from Gina's storeroom. Witches didn't have much power over ghosts, but magic still worked in the presence of spookies as long as you weren't trying to directly affect the ghost itself. The plastic was thin, and I could feel the liquid inside sloshing around. I raised my hand high and threw the ball down as hard as I could.

The ball hit the floor and split open, and I heard the satisfying hiss as the spilling liquid became a gas. At first there were just a few red tendrils of light coming up from the floor where the ball had struck, but soon the red lights grew until the room was illuminated in an eerie crimson.

I turned to Nick. "Let there be light." I'm not sure being able to see the room comforted him much, because I noted that his hand stayed clutching the back of my jacket. I faced the center of the room. "Come on, Doc! We don't have all night!"

Neither, apparently, did he. I don't know if there was actually a whooshing sound as he suddenly appeared or if my mind just supplied it, but in less than a second, he was there, taller than was possible and black in dress as well as demeanor. He towered over Nick and me by at least a foot, and rage emanated off of him. His eyes blazed red as he flicked his hand toward me.

With just that gesture, he sent me flying. I felt like a wrecking ball had hit me. As I was airborne, I thought, *Oh, this is going to hurt.* And I was right. I hit the wall and crumpled to the floor, the impact sending jolts of pain through my body. The jolt nearly made me lose consciousness, and for a moment, everything went black. I shook my head and tried to take a deep breath. Mistake. Pain shot through my chest, telling me I'd cracked a rib, at the very least. I shook my head, trying to regroup. I knew during my short tumble through the air I'd lost my grip on the shotgun, and I looked through the red haze to locate it.

"Shit! Duncan!" Nick's scream filled the room, even over the ghostly wind. I looked over to see that he was batting at something down at his feet with the barrel of his shotgun, and it took me a moment to realize hands were reaching up from the floor, grabbing at his legs. There must have been a dozen of them, all white and so thin they were nearly skeletal, jutting up from the floorboards. Most were just visible from the wrist up, but a few—those closest to Nick's legs—were longer, nearly to the elbow. All of the fingers were blindly grasping. One hand had a hold on the back of Nick's pant leg and was attempting to pull him down, or at least throw him off balance. Others were holding on to his shoes and the cuffs of his pants.

Nick's thrusts with the shotgun didn't seem to have any effect on the spectral hands. In fact, more often than not, he was simply smashing the barrel against his own shins. His face, lit by the crimson witch light, was a mask of sheer terror. "Duncan!" he screamed. "Help!"

I spotted my shotgun lying several feet away. Instinctively, I reached out for it, ignoring the sharp pain that shot through my chest as I moved. I'm not sure what I planned on doing with the gun, since firing it at the hands would probably dispel the ghostly appendages but would just as likely hit Nick. Still, I didn't have time to think, and in situations like that, having a gun in your mitts is better than not having a gun in your mitts.

It didn't matter. By the time I scooped up the shotgun, a bright light shot out from the floor around Nick and the hands seemed to draw in enough energy to pull Nick down. He yelled out, and the light momentarily was so bright that I had to shield my eyes. I could barely make out Nick, falling through the floorboards with the hands assisting his descent. In seconds, he was only visible from the waist up, and then he rapidly disappeared from view. When he was gone, there was a whoosh in the air, and the light—and the hole—was no more.

I had the shotgun in my hands, though, and I shot a quick glance at the specter of Dr. Moore, who was gazing at the spot where Nick had been seconds before. The bastard had a smug, pleased look on his face that made me forget the shooting pains making it hard for me to draw anything other than shallow breaths. Before the doctor could react, I had the shotgun aimed right at his ugly mug.

"Fuck off!" I yelled as I fired both barrels.

I half expected the shots to have no effect. After all, old Doc Moore seemed to be super spook, having abilities and powers I'd never encountered with a ghost before. It wouldn't have surprised me to find the rock salt would simply go through Moore, and then he'd turn and send me flying again, or something worse. Thankfully, though, the shots did the trick. As soon as the pellets hit Moore, he was gone. Immediately, the spectral wind died down, and I found myself in an empty bedroom. I felt like kissing the shotgun barrel, and might have if it wouldn't have burned my lips.

"Nice to know that the old standbys still work," I muttered as I slowly got to my feet. My ribs felt like they were on fire, and several words my Aunt Connie would have blushed upon hearing escaped my mouth as I awkwardly got upright. Keeping my right elbow tight against my side seemed to help, as it reminded me not to take too deep a breath.

I reached out with my psychic sense, or as Robbie called it, my "Spidey sense," but could detect no paranormal activity in the room. I went over to where Nick had disappeared through the floorboards. The room was still being lit by Gina's witch light, but there were no marks on the wood, nothing to show someone had just been sucked through. Nick's shotgun was lying there, though. Whatever had pulled him down had found the salt-loaded weapon too difficult to swallow, so to speak.

I looked up and addressed Doc Moore. He wasn't in the room, but I guessed he was close enough to hear me. "If you've harmed one hair on Nick's head, I'm going to send you to hell so fast that Satan won't have time to stamp your passport." It wasn't the wittiest quip I'd ever threatened a spirit with, but my ribs were screaming, and it was the best I could come up with on the spot.

Okay, so Nick had gone through the floor, pulled by spectral hands. It made sense, in a weird sort of way, that he might now be downstairs. I started to leave the room and realized it wasn't just my ribs that were damaged. My left leg wasn't broken—at least I didn't think it was—but it didn't want to work properly either. I limped slowly out of the room, my right arm plastered against my ribs and the shotgun in my left. Yeah, watch out, nasty ghosts. I'm a badass. I'll get ya. Just don't move too fast.

Going down the stairs was fun. I stopped after a couple of steps to hiss loudly and utter a few more choice words. The thought of Nick somewhere in the house needing my help spurred me on. Behind me, the witch light was beginning to lose some of its mojo, but there was enough red glow coming from the room that I could navigate without killing myself. I pressed my butt against the stair rail and used it to steady my descent.

I got down the stairs after what seemed a decade and limped my way to the living room, which would have been directly under where Nick had vanished. The room was dark, but I could see enough to tell that he wasn't there. "Nick?" I yelled. "If you can hear me, a shout-out would be appreciated!"

The house was silent. I could sense our good doctor was somewhere in the background, licking his wounds, but not much else. I listened, hoping to hear some knock or scratching sound or anything that would tell me where Nick was. Nothing.

"Okay," I said aloud, "if he's not here, maybe the basement."

More stairs. Lovely. My leg was behaving a little better now, and I was pretty sure I'd somehow managed to twist my ankle as I'd fallen, and while I was still limping, it wasn't quite as Lon Chaney Jr. as the Mummy as it had been. I found the door leading down to the basement and used my right hand to open it. The shotgun, even though both barrels had been fired, wasn't leaving my left hand. I'd bean the damned ghost over the head with it if I had to.

The basement, of course, was pitch-black. I hesitated at the top of the steps. "Nick? You down there?"

I didn't expect an answer, so I was surprised when a small voice replied, "Yeah."

"Are you okay?"

There was a pause. "I'm okay. I'm covered in goo, though."

"Hang on. I'll be right down."

"Duncan?"

"Yeah?"

"I want a raise."

Despite the pain in my side, I smiled at that. "I wasn't aware you were even on the payroll."

"Yeah. About that."

I didn't want to try to get down the basement stairs in pitch-blackness, so I fished the flashlight out of my jacket pocket. I really didn't expect it to work, but a press of the button gave me a good, steady beam. Maybe old Doc Moore was off cooling his heels and wasn't using any of his energy-sucking mojo. I found a light switch and flicked it. Sure enough, a bare bulb down at the bottom of the stairs came to life. "Let there be light," I said as I turned off the flashlight and returned it to my pocket.

I decided to chance it and leaned the shotgun against the wall at the top of the stairs. It was empty, in any case, and I really wanted both hands available to hold on to the rail and anything else I could grab onto. Still, it was tough going, and my groaning and occasional expletive told Nick that all wasn't well. That and the fact that it was taking ages for me to get down fifteen steps.

"Duncan, are you all right?"

I winced as I went down the last stair. "Fine. Good. Great. May have a few bruises. Couple cracked ribs. Oh, and I twisted my ankle."

"How did you do that?"

I still couldn't see Nick, but his voice was coming from the area beneath the stairs. I could see one wall that held a bunch of cupboards and shelves and another that had a washer and dryer. There was a pile of dirty laundry piled on the floor in front of the washing machine. "Oh, I hit a wall."

"Why did you do that?"

"I was airborne. I had to hit something." I limped around the stairs. Nick was huddled against the wall there, looking exhausted. As he'd said, he was covered in a green glob. He'd done his best to wipe the slimy crap off his face, but he still looked a mess.

"What is this stuff?"

"Ectoplasm. Haven't you seen *Ghostbusters?*"

He wiped a hand across his cheek, but it really just smeared the thick gel. He chuckled mirthlessly. "I'll never watch it again, that's for sure. At least not the same way."

Other than being coated with ectoplasm, Nick didn't seem to be harmed. I reached out my left hand and helped him to his feet. "What happened to you? Last I saw, a bunch of hands were dragging you through the floor."

Nick ran a hand over his hair, getting a handful of glop, which he flung against the wall. There was a puddle of the stuff where he'd been lying. "I'm not really sure. There was this bright light, and I think there were figures—ghosts of young men. They were all over me, grabbing at me and pulling me right through the house. I ended up here, screaming my ass off, when suddenly, they just disappeared."

"I bet that was me. I shot Doc Moore with rock salt. They probably were the spirits of his victims. He's still commanding them, even after death. Bastard's got his own little ghostly army. When he got zapped, his hold over them vanished, and so did they."

"So," Nick said slowly, "what now?"

"We get you washed off and me patched up. Then we go to Plan B."

"And Plan B is?"

I shrugged. "Shit if I know."

CHAPTER 7

"AND YOU did this how?" Gina asked as she tightened the bindings around my chest.

"Ow. Does it have to be so tight?"

"They're treated with a special healing tincture," she said in that "stop being such a baby" tone evil nurses around the world have down pat. "This stuff should have your ribs healed by the morning, but yes, it has to be tight. Why? You can still breathe, can't you?"

"Well, yes, but…. I feel like I'm wearing a corset or something."

"Then pretend that you're William Shatner, suck in your gut, and smile for the cameras." She finished her ministrations and stepped back to examine her work. "Done. You can put your shirt back on now."

When I grunted trying to get my right arm through the sleeve, Gina emitted an exasperated sigh but helped me into my shirt. "Thanks," I said as I began buttoning it up.

"Next time, maybe you should take me along," she said. "Witches and ghosts don't mix very well, but at least I can help so that you don't end up killing yourself."

"I didn't do it myself. I had help. He threw me against a wall. I didn't really notice at the time, what with cracking my ribs and Nick being pulled into the floorboards, but I'm betting there's a Duncan-sized indentation in the plaster."

We were at my place, with the early-morning sun beaming in from the windows. I was sitting on the couch with Daisy curled up next to me. Robbie was still too weak to make an appearance, but I could feel that he was nearby. I'd called Gina pretty early, as I'd spent a fairly sleepless night after returning from Jason Church's house, because every time I shifted, I wanted to scream. I could, of course, have gone to the emergency room at Wishard Hospital, but when you showed up all bruised and broken, they tended to ask how it happened, and I really didn't think they wanted to hear that a ghost had thrashed the hell out of me. Also, Gina's cures acted much, much faster. It was nice having a healing witch for a friend.

Gina stowed some extra bandages she hadn't used and several bottles into her big black bag on the coffee table. "There's something else bothering you. You haven't looked me in the eye the whole time I've been here."

"Wasn't aware that was a prerequisite," I said. I opened my peepers wide and glared at her. "There. Satisfied?"

She arched an eyebrow. "Come clean. This isn't just about this ghost. What's up?"

The truth was that as soon as Gina left, I planned on going to Dr. Mark Callahan's office and having it out with her boyfriend, but I didn't want her to know anything about Elton the Demon's allegations until I talked with Mark. "Nothing," I said.

"It's about Robbie, isn't it? You've got some plan to talk him out of crossing over, and you don't want me to talk you out of it."

Well, no, that wasn't it at all, but it was a better conversation than telling her that her boyfriend was probably part of a group devoted to wiping witches off the face of the earth. "I don't have a plan," I said. "As such."

One was forming, though. I felt a bit guilty even thinking about it, but I quickly rationalized my motives because I wouldn't be lying, not even a teensy bit. Still, I was using an unfair advantage. You know that feeling you get when you're talking with someone, and you're absolutely sure someone's listening at the keyhole? I was getting that. Only this person wasn't at a keyhole; he was just invisible and a little distant. But I was betting he could hear us.

Gina sat down on the couch so Daisy was in between us. She snaked an arm around my shoulder. "I know," she said softly, "that you love him. But he's been dead more than ten years now. You need a relationship with someone you can touch, feel, make love with. It won't be easy, but in time, you'll move on."

"You think?" I said tonelessly.

"I know." She pulled me a little closer to her so my head was cradled against her outstretched arm. Daisy, disturbed by the movement, lifted her head and snorted. Satisfied we weren't going to interrupt her morning siesta further, she went back to snoozing. Gina looked up at the ceiling as if she were seeing the future being played out there. "Eventually, you'll find someone else. Not right away, of course. But in time. Maybe even Nick. You've always found him attractive, and you've told me several times that you wonder what it would be like between the two of you."

"Yeah, I wonder," I replied. "But the actual truth of the matter is that I know what would happen."

"What's that?"

"Even if I waited until the hurt from Robbie's leaving wasn't so strong, if I tried to have a relationship with anyone, Nick included, it would end in disaster."

A tiny frown furrowed Gina's brow. "What do you mean?"

I lifted my head off her arm and sat up straight, composing my thoughts. I wanted to make sure my words came out just right, so I let the pause drag a moment. "If I dated anyone, even Nick, it would last a few months. Tops. Eventually, though, I'd realize they aren't Robbie, and it would end. And Nick's become a good friend. I wouldn't want to put him through that. Plus, it would kill our friendship."

"Well," Gina said, "you say that now, but—"

"No. It's the reality."

She shook her head gently. "It wouldn't be Robbie, of course. But you'd learn to love them in their own way."

I needed something to do with my hands, so I stroked Daisy as she slumbered. The dog's tail twitched, but other than that, she didn't stir. "I don't think I would. I think I was made for just one person, and that person is Robbie."

"So you're saying that you'd stay celibate the rest of your life? Once he moves on, that's it? No more love for Duncan?"

"Hey, don't knock celibacy. I've got a master's degree."

"But...." Gina didn't seem to know what to say. She shook her head and let the word hang.

"It's kind of like George and Gracie," I said.

Gina's frown deepened. "The humpback whales in *Star Trek 4*?"

"No, the real people they were named after, the radio comedians George Burns and Gracie Allen. After she died, he never remarried or even had a lasting relationship with another woman. He often said that Gracie was the only woman in the world for him, and anything else would just be a pale imitation."

A slight smile formed on Gina's lips. "Are you George or Gracie in this analogy?"

"Doesn't matter. I'm just saying that Robbie is it for me. After him, there's nothing."

Gina patted my shoulder. "Give it time. And he's not planning on crossing over until New Year's. You've got time."

I was hoping I had more than a few months, but I just shrugged. "I know me. And there's no doubt in my mind how things will play out."

"That's nice," Gina said. "But sad. I hate to think of you being without someone."

"The sadness started over ten years ago when Robbie died. But," I said, plastering a smile on my lips, "we've had a great ride. It would have been wonderful to see what our lives would have been like if he'd lived, but, as things are, I'm glad I've just had this extra time with him. I wouldn't have wanted it any other way."

I almost felt a movement in the room, over by the hallway, as if someone unseen was lurking there. I just hoped I wasn't laying it on too thick. Time would tell.

Gina sighed and stood. "Well, I'd better go and check on Nick. I told him I'd drop by, although he said he wasn't as injured as you. Bruises on his legs, he said."

"Yeah. He was hitting himself with the stock of his shotgun."

Gina hefted her oversized black bag. "You guys really need to find something else to do with your nights. Or I'm going to have to invest in a hell of a lot more magic supplies."

I BURST into the waiting room like a man on a mission, which I was. Because of Nurse Gina's wonderful spells and potions, I no longer had a limp, although I still had the tight wrap around my chest holding my healing ribs in place. I moved quickly, scanning the room. Three people waiting. A mother and two brats. Behind a glass partition was a receptionist. When I didn't approach her and instead started for the inner door, she quickly slid her window open.

"Sir?" she asked, a hint of worry in her voice. I must not have looked happy. "Excuse me, sir, but do you have an appointment?"

"I do," I shot back. "Hold all of Dr. Callahan's calls."

She rose from her chair. "Sir! You can't go in there!"

I pushed open the door. "I think you'll find that I can," I replied.

Inside, Mark the Dentist was bent over a middle-aged woman. She saw me first and started to say something, but moving her mouth with Mark poised over her face with a sharp instrument wasn't a good idea. She gagged out a protest, causing Mark to turn to see me storming in.

I looked at the shocked woman. "If you'll excuse us for a moment. The doctor and I have something to discuss."

Behind me, the receptionist had joined the party. She was a young gal, maybe in her midtwenties. She didn't seem to know how to handle a big guy wearing a leather jacket bursting in on a teeth cleaning. Understandably, she was flustered. "Should I call the police?"

Mark looked from her to me and then back to her. I wondered if he caught sight of the .38 in the holster under my jacket. He certainly saw the manila envelope in my hands. "It's okay, Jill. I know this gentleman."

I wasn't feeling much like a gentleman, and I'm pretty sure I didn't look like one. I felt like a thundercloud. Glaring at the woman in the dentist chair, I said, "You can leave now. Rinse and spit if you have to, but you'll have to reschedule your appointment. Possibly with another dentist."

The woman hesitated, started to get off the chair, and then realized she was still wearing the dental bib. "Should I take this off?"

"I would. It doesn't really go with your outfit."

She fumbled with the clasp but finally got the thing from around her neck. She looked at Mark for instructions but got none—he was staring at me—so she dropped the bib on the chair and made for the door. She went out and the receptionist started to go as well, but she stopped one last time. "Are you sure…?"

Mark nodded. "It's okay. You'd better send the people out there waiting home. Reschedule them. Cancel the rest of my appointments today as well. Tell them an emergency has come up." He eyed me. "I'm assuming this is an emergency?"

"You could say that."

To the receptionist, Mark said, "Then take the rest of the day off."

She slowly backed out of the room, closing the door behind her, all the while looking at me like I was a crazed terrorist, which, from her point of view, was not far from the truth. When the door had latched and we were alone, I tossed the envelope on the vacated dental chair.

Mark frowned. "What's this?"

"Open it."

I noticed Mark's hand trembled a little as he reached out and grabbed the envelope. "I don't understand," he said as he pulled out the photographs and articles. He began to examine the items more carefully, especially the photographs. After a moment, he glanced at me. "What are these?"

"I think you know."

He shook his head. "These are doctored. Photoshopped. Something. I don't—"

I had my gun out and covered the few feet between us before he had time to react. I pushed him against the wall and pressed the muzzle of the .38 against his cheek. "Now think very carefully," I said, "before you make your next statement, because it could be your last."

"I don't know what's going on! What are those pictures? I don't—"

Some people are good liars. Some aren't. Mark Callahan wasn't. His left eye gave a little twitch, plus the pitch of his voice wasn't right. If he really had no idea what was going on, he'd be more panicked, desperate. To me, it came across that he was protesting just to give himself time to think. I grabbed hold of the front of his smock and jabbed the muzzle into his cheek. He was plastered against the wall, and I shoved up against him so he had no room to squirm. "Save it. You've got one minute to tell me everything about this cult of yours, or your brains are going to be splattered all over your nice white walls."

Now he was genuinely worried. He tried to speak, but only a little squeak came out. Trying again, he muttered, "You wouldn't shoot me."

"Look into my face. I think you'll see that I wouldn't hesitate. You fuck with my friends, and you fuck with me, and I'm not someone you want to fuck with. Now talk."

Sweat was forming on his forehead, and his eyes were wet with tears. "It's not what you think!"

"Then what is it?"

A couple of the tears rolled down his cheek. "We... we knew there was a witch somewhere in Indianapolis. We suspected that it was Gina, but we weren't sure."

"Go on."

"Can you put the gun away?"

"I don't think so. Go on."

"I was supposed to get close to her, find out if she was really a witch. We figured it was the only way to learn for sure—"

"What the hell does it matter?" I growled. "What do you care?"

"They aren't human! I know she looks like a regular person, but she isn't! They're like a biological offshoot, a remnant from ancient times! There aren't many of them left, but the Order is—"

"Yeah, killing them off. I gathered that. Why?" I was angry as hell but also a little sad. Mark the Dentist had seemed like such a nice guy.

He tried to move, so I gave him just enough leeway and then slammed him back against the wall, hard enough that jars and other items in a cabinet near us rattled. I shifted the gun so the muzzle was now under his right nostril, just to remind him it was still there. In a small, pleading voice, he said, "You think she's a good person, I know. And she seems to be. But they have powers that you wouldn't believe. They go against God's will, and—"

I fought the urge to belt him with the butt of the gun. "You and your cronies are murdering bastards, from what I can see. I don't think you have the right to speak of God's will."

"Witches are evil! You have to see that!"

As my ribs were tightly bound by bandages that were healing me as we spoke, I didn't have to think about that one. "You know Gina isn't. She's good. There may be a few of her kind—"

"That's just it!" He was sobbing now. "I admit, I haven't found anything she's done that was evil, but it's still against God's will, and—"

"Like you know God's will."

"Eventually she'll turn evil. They all do! I can show you documents! My people have—"

He was shouting now, and the receptionist must have overheard his cries because there was a tentative knock at the door. "Dr. Callahan? Are you okay?" she asked.

"Fine! Fine!" He shouted unconvincingly. He sounded like a guy with a gun shoved halfway up his nose, even to me. There was a pause, and then the receptionist's footsteps went away from the door, probably to get to the nearest phone to call 911. I could imagine the call. *Hello. There's a maniac threatening Dr. Callahan. I think he's got a gun. He's devilishly handsome, but I think he's dangerous.*

Okay, maybe she'd leave out the handsome part.

I got a tighter grip on Mark's smock. "Come on," I said. "We're going for a ride."

I THINK Mark figured he'd get a chance to get away, and that's why he agreed to leave with me so easily. Well, the gun poked into his back may have done a little convincing as well. When we got out to the lobby, we found it empty, which I was sort of expecting. The young receptionist was gone, obviously after having notified the authorities there was a madman in the Chase building downtown, holding a poor dentist captive on the fifth floor. I half expected to find about a dozen cops with guns drawn waiting for us when we exited the elevator, but no.

I had taken off my jacket and had it draped over my arm so it hid the gun I was holding on Mark. He walked a few feet ahead of me as we made our way to the main entrance, and while I couldn't see his eyes with his back to me, I knew he was darting his glance from left to right, hoping someone would figure out he was being marched out against his will. No one did. We even passed the armed guard at the security desk without incident. I smiled at the guard. He smiled back.

My car was parked on Meridian Street, just outside Mark's building. The meter had run out and the flag was up, but no ticket was shoved under my windshield wiper. Mark started for the passenger door, but I shook my head. "You're driving," I said.

"But…!" He wanted to protest, but it was hard to trump a .38 pointed at you. At least he'd stopped crying and slobbering. There was a bit of a wet stain on his pants, though, where he'd peed himself upstairs. He was still wearing his dentist smock, and I hadn't let him grab a coat, so he was shivering a little. Whether it was from the chilliness of the air or the fact that I might shoot him at any moment was anybody's guess.

He got behind the wheel, and I sat next to him, keeping him covered every moment. I tossed him the keys. "If I were you," I said, "I would drive carefully and slowly. Don't make any sudden moves or try anything tricky. You'd be dead before you knew it."

As we pulled away, I heard the police sirens approaching. Unluckily for Mark, we got into the flow of traffic and had turned the corner, and still no squad cars appeared to save his ass. I would admit, though, that from how near the sirens sounded, it was a close one.

I had Mark drive us out of the city, through the suburb of Avon, and beyond. Finally, we came to a road that looked like it didn't lead much of anywhere. I told Mark to take it. We wound around some country roads until I found a nice little area that looked like a perfect place for a chat, a small woods in between two cornfields. I told Mark to pull over, which he did.

We hadn't said much during the drive, even though Mark had tried to start a conversation several times. His queries as to what I was planning, however, met with a stony silence. I didn't want anything to distract me from watching him and his driving. If he had tried anything, such as wrecking the car or running a red light to bring attention to us, I wouldn't have shot him. I didn't think. But he didn't know that, so we got out to our secluded spot with no mishaps.

We got out of the car, and I motioned for him to go over and sit on a rock shaded by several trees. We were out in the boondocks, but there was always the chance a car might drive by, and I didn't want them seeing us. I stood several yards away, and while I didn't point the gun at Mark, I didn't stow it back into the holster either.

There, with the leaves falling around us and a distant autumn sun shining down on the scene, he told me his story. It seemed membership into the Order of Cotton Mather, at least for the Callahans, was a family affair. His father had been a member, and as far as Mark knew, his grandfather had been too, and on down the line.

Mark sat on the rock with his head down. He was no longer afraid of me, or at least wasn't visibly shaking. In fact, he seemed to be relieved to get his secret off his chest.

At first, Mark had just thought it was sort of a joke society, a bunch of guys who went on about the evil of witches and how they should be destroyed. Every now and then his father, who was a plumber, would take off for a week or so, but Mark had assumed this was just for a gathering of the group where they would drink and party and generally behave badly. The witch stuff, he thought, was just a cover story.

When he was seventeen, though, his father took him to his first witch hunt.

"They had found one in Georgia, in a little town called Ringold." Mark was examining his fingernails as he talked, as if they were intensely fascinating. "Living in a mobile home on the outside of town. We met up at an inn in town. One of the members, Randy Peterson, had moved into the town about a month before to gather his evidence. Randy was retired and had some money stashed away, so it was easy for him to relocate whenever the Order needed him to."

"How many members are there?" I asked.

Mark shook his head. "I don't know. They work in small groups, and only the leaders of individual groups have any contact with each other. There were six in our group. Still are, actually, although the roster has changed over the years."

"What happened with this woman in Georgia?" I realized I was speaking in hushed tones. It seemed like that kind of conversation. Or maybe I felt some reverence was due to this unknown woman from Ringold.

"We went out to her home late one night. The other guys pulled her screaming from her house. Then we took her out to a field where they had already prepared at funeral pyre. They tied her to a stake and burned her. I remember hearing her screams in my dreams for months after that."

"How do you know she was a witch and not just some poor woman you guys torched?"

"Peterson had done his investigation well. There had been several times, over the years, when someone had argued with the woman—"

"She had a name," I interrupted. "What was it?"

Mark sighed and seemed reluctant to say it. Finally, he went on. "Miranda Soames. Anyway, it seems several times that people who had words with her mysteriously died shortly after. While Peterson was down there, the bank was threatening to foreclose on her mobile home due to lack of payments. About a week after Peterson moved into town, the bank manager died from falling down a flight of stairs."

I said, "Coincidence."

"Peterson took photographs of Soames performing a black mass. She foolishly hadn't closed the curtains in her windows, and he could see her performing the ritual. I saw the pictures myself. She somehow had collected a lock from the bank manager's hair and had attached it to a crude doll. She twisted the head of the doll, and the next morning the manager was found dead, his neck broken from the fall."

Okay, she didn't sound like the nicest of people. "One evil witch doesn't mean they all are."

Mark shook his head. "That's just it. They aren't human. Gina could be hundreds of years old. They don't age like humans. They can even change their appearance. She appears to be a young woman with blonde hair, but I bet in the past she's appeared as an older woman or even a child. You can't trust anything about them."

I pursed my lips. "Actually, I can. I've known Gina for years. She's a good person. Wouldn't harm a hair on anyone's head."

Mark grimaced. "If you'd seen the things I have...."

"I'll wager I've seen things you haven't dreamed of," I said. "Tell me. If someone showed you a child and said that the child had the possibility of growing up to be the next Hitler, what would you do?"

"It's not the same thing."

"No? Has Gina done anything evil? Has she ever harmed anyone?"

"Not yet, but—"

"No buts. If you go after someone because they have powers, they're different, they're not, as you say, entirely human... if you destroy someone just because of those things, even if that person has never done anything wrong, then you're the evil one. Not them. End of story."

Mark's shoulders slumped even more than they had been. I could tell he wasn't convinced by my arguments, but that didn't really matter to me. I shook my head as I watched him. I recalled the time Gina had been in a coma. Mark had been at the hospital almost constantly. Had that all been a sham? Had he been waiting for her to miraculously come out of it? The concern he'd shown then had seemed genuine to me. In retrospect, though, I'd never seen them kiss. Never seen them hold hands. I wondered how much of the relationship Gina had imagined. Usually, she was a good judge of character. In love, it seemed, we all rushed in with blinders on.

"Look," I went on. "This is over. You're out of your little cult. You won't have any contact with Gina ever again. You're going to move out of Indianapolis. You're going to tell your little friends that Gina isn't a witch, that your information was wrong. You're going—"

"It's too late," Mark said weakly.

I stared at him. "What do you mean?"

"I've already reported to the members of the Order. Several weeks ago. A plan to dispose of her is already underway."

My blood seemed to freeze in my veins. "What?"

Mark looked like he might start blubbering again, and I couldn't blame him. His words were riling me up again. "I was pretty sure that we were correct and that Gina was a witch, but I didn't have any evidence. Then, when she and I went to Salem for a vacation, she told me everything. She told me she was a witch." He rubbed a hand over his mouth. "They've already begun to arrive. Three of them are already in town. When everyone is here, they'll act."

"Act?"

He sniffed and glanced up at me. It was the first time since he'd sat down on the rock that he'd made eye contact. "They'll burn her."

I forced myself to count to ten. Actually, I only made it to four, but it helped calm me down a little. "Okay," I said slowly, "in that case, there's something you're going to do for me. After you do it, you're going to disappear. If I ever hear that you're doing anything like this again, I'll put a bullet right through your excuse for a brain. You're going to move away and not have any contact with your little buddies. I'll keep tabs on you. You'll live quietly, but you'll live. Savvy?"

He looked miserable. "What do you want me to do?"

I told him.

CHAPTER 8

"YOU SURE you're up to this?" I asked.

Robbie cocked an eye at me. It was accompanied by a sarcastic twist of the lip. "I'm good. But then, I just had the energy zapped out of me the last time we were here. I didn't sail through the room and go splat against a wall."

We were in Jason Church's house, milling about the kitchen. Well, I was milling about. Robbie was sitting at the small dining table. He was, to be fair, pretty solid and healthy looking. He was wearing a Colts football jersey under his high school letter jacket and well-worn jeans. His hair was mussed and sticking up in places, which never made sense to me. He could appear in any clothes he wore while he was alive and could give the impression of being perfectly groomed if he so wished. Why not make the extra effort and have combed hair? He had, on many occasions, explained to me that it was easier to look like he felt. So he must have been feeling all messy haired. Even after a lifetime of dealing with ghosts, there was a lot I didn't understand. Personally, I went nowhere with messy hair.

It was the middle of the afternoon. After leaving Mark Callahan, I'd run some errands and arranged a thing or two, but I'd rushed to get things done so I could get the feel of the Church house during the day. There was no guarantee old Doc Moore wouldn't rear his ugly head during daylight hours, but according to Jason, the paranormal activity went on mostly at night, so I wanted to see if the house had a different feel while the sun was still out.

And, for the most part, it felt like any other house on a cold November day. But there was an underlying something, a little nag in the back of my mind, telling me danger was lurking close by and I shouldn't let my guard down even for a second.

I paced the kitchen, letting my senses stretch out. To help concentration, I closed my eyes briefly. I pictured the tiles I was walking on, the wall, the refrigerator. I could see them all in my mind's eye. And there was something more there. It was as if every board, every appliance, every thread of carpet in the house, was infected. Doctor Moore's evil was a cancer, and it coated everything around him.

Opening my eyes, I paused to look at the spirit sitting slumped in the chair at the table. Somehow, seeing Robbie like that made me remember our first Thanksgiving together. He'd insisted on taking me to his parents' house for the annual feast. I hadn't met Mr. and Mrs. Church before. They had been nice, if a little reserved. They were still getting used to the idea that their beloved son had a boyfriend. We had been twenty years old. When the call to dinner came, Robbie had made sure we had seats together and had slumped down just as he was sitting now. His mother had told him to sit up straight and to stop, as she'd said, "sitting on his spine."

I smiled at him. "You're sitting on your spine again."

Robbie rolled his eyes in mock exasperation but corrected his posture. "Better, Mom?"

"Much." I walked over to the kitchen counter and placed my hand on the surface, certain I'd pick up some residual evil Moore had left behind. Sure enough, it felt like a typical porcelain counter, but in the background was… something black, something not right. Someone with even a little psychic sense, like Jason, must have found living in the house a constant source of fear. Everything he touched must have put him on edge.

I sighed. "I think Dr. Moore must have been planning this for a very long time. It's almost like he's become the house. Everything has his psychic stench on it. Maybe that's how he has so much power. He's built a battery for himself, so to speak. Now he gets energy from the house itself." I shook my head. "I still don't understand how he does it. I've never encountered a ghost that could knock me off my feet with just a gesture before. He's unnaturally strong."

Robbie scratched at his temple. "Where is he buried?"

"I don't know. I don't think it came up in Nick's research. I'll have to ask him."

"And Nick thinks that the hands that pulled him through the floorboards, the figures he encountered, were Dr. Moore's victims?"

"He wasn't sure. Granted, at the time, he was scared out of his wits, but he got that impression. Which begs the question, why would Moore's victims help him out? You'd think they'd be against him and be on our side."

"Maybe they were," Robbie said. "Maybe they were pulling Nick away, getting him out of Moore's reach."

I pondered that, pursing my lips and nodding my head. "I hadn't thought of that. You could be right. Good thinking."

"Hey, I'm not just a pretty face."

"Nick said that he felt they were interrupted, though. That if I hadn't pelted Moore with salt, they would have continued and pulled him even farther, down into the ground under the house."

"Well, he was really scared at the time. Nick could be wrong about that."

"If they weren't helping Nick, then we have to assume that Moore's using some influence over them. They're his own private army. If that's the case, then we have an even bigger problem here. Moore's malevolent influence, in addition to the negative power from his victims. They died horribly, leaving behind dark energy. Now, they're all feeding off each other, plus the infection of the house itself." I snapped my fingers. The sudden sound made Robbie start. "Sorry. But that makes sense. Moore's made this place his fortress. He's slowly spread his evil—for want of a better word—into the very foundation of the house. He's somehow found a way to control the spirits of his victims. They feed off the energy of the house as well, but only as much as Moore allows them."

"Could be." Robbie nodded.

"And when he saw you—bam! He grabs your energy as well!"

"So," Robbie said pensively, "you're saying he's like a psychic vacuum cleaner."

"More than that." I smiled at Robbie's attempt at humor. "He gathers the energy but then distributes it all over the house. It's there, in the floorboards, in the cabinets, in the walls. He can draw on it anytime he wants. He has so much power at his fingertips that he can do almost anything."

"Great," Robbie said with a false smile. "Which means it's going to be really, really hard to get rid of him."

"We'll find a way. We always do. Batman and Robin. Holmes and Watson. Duncan and Robbie. When a team is unbeatable, nothing, even a supercharged pissy ghost, can stop them."

I hoped I wasn't laying it on too thick, and I sneaked a surreptitious glance at Robbie. His lip was twisted in thought, and he seemed pensive. "Duncan," he said slowly.

"Yeah."

"You know how I said that I wanted to move…. Shit, do you feel that?"

I did, and I cursed Doc Moore for his bad timing. There was suddenly a feeling in the air, the kind you feel when a really bad thunderstorm is about to hit. The sun was still shining outside, but the room grew noticeably darker. I could even feel the hairs on the back of my neck prickle. "We're about to have company."

Robbie nodded. "I think you're right."

"Let's get out of here," I said, already heading for the doorway.

"We're going to run?" Robbie's eyes bugged out.

"Tactical retreat. We've learned some things from being here, and we need to formulate a plan. Tangling with Big Ugly right now won't solve anything, and I don't want him zapping the energy out of you again. We just got you back up to snuff."

Robbie rose from his chair. "Plus, you're still healing. It wouldn't be good for you to go splat against a wall again."

"True."

Robbie grinned. "We rationalized that pretty good, didn't we?"

"Sure as shit did. Now, are you going to wag your jaw all afternoon, or are we going to get the hell out of Dodge?"

Robbie followed me through the house to the front door. As we walked—briskly but not at a full-out run, so we didn't look like we were frightened kittens rushing away from a big, bad dog—not only the light in the house dimmed, but the very walls, ceilings, and floors darkened perceptively. It was as if the building was decaying and aging as we moved. I was almost surprised when I flung open the front door to find the clouds weren't obscuring the sun. As I closed the door behind us, muffled laughter could be heard coming from the foyer.

"We'll be back," I said, with more bravado than I felt.

We turned to head down the porch steps, and Robbie asked, "Would Batman have run away like that?"

"Which Batman are we talking about? Christian Bale, Michael Keaton, Adam West, or one of the other guys?"

"There's only one Batman."

"I guess you're right."

We were now going at a good clip away from the house, my footsteps clicking on the concrete path that led from the front of the house down to the sidewalk. "Adam West," we said at the same time.

I said it as a joke. Robbie, I'm not so sure of. He had weird tastes. Which could explain how he'd put up with me all these years.

"WE NEED to talk," I said.

"Hello to you too, Duncan," Gina replied. She gestured for me to come inside. The smile on her face vanished when she saw I wasn't exactly happy. "What's wrong?"

I stepped inside, and she closed the door behind me. I sighed, more to give myself time to think of how to begin than anything else. I slowly took off my leather jacket to buy even more time. "I…." Good start. But where to go from there?

Gina touched my arm, her concern evident. "Duncan, tell me. What's going on?"

I sighed again. Sighing was good. Maybe I could have the entire conversation using only sighs. Gina could ask me questions, and I could reply with one sigh for yes and two for no. Or maybe I could just man up and tell her. "It's about Mark."

"Mark? Mark Callahan? Is he all right?"

I motioned toward her parlor. "Let's go sit down. And alcohol would be nice. This isn't going to be pleasant."

I HAD been sitting on my own in Gina's parlor for nearly an hour. I thought about turning on the television or the radio just to have noise of some sort, but that would mean getting up off the couch, and I didn't feel like moving. After I'd told Gina about Mark and the Order of Cotton Mather—a group she was all too familiar with, although she'd never mentioned them to me—she had wanted some alone time. It wasn't that she didn't believe me, but she wanted to go to the little room where she entertained her clients for her fortune-telling business. A consultation with her crystal ball was in order, and maybe a reading of her tarot cards. And, I guessed, a few bitter or angry tears.

I was just getting to the point where I wondered if I should go and check on her when she came back into the room. Her eyes were red, but there were no current tears. She sat down on the couch next to me, keeping her pretty face low and avoiding my eyes.

She was sitting slightly forward, so I put a hand on her back and gave her a little massage. She was silent for over a minute. Finally, she said, "I don't see how I could have been so blind."

"Not just you," I said softly. "None of us thought there was anything amiss about him."

"But I should have known. I was dating him!" She closed her eyes tightly and then opened them and let an exasperated groan escape her lips. "Now, of course, I can see that there were signs. I should have seen them."

"You were in love. Love tends to blind us."

She nodded. "Yes, but—"

"Plus," I added, "I think he really did have some affection for you. Back when you were in the hospital, he showed genuine concern. I'm sure part of him, at least, was falling for you."

"But he was waiting to see if I would do something to prove to him and his stupid cult that I was a witch. And what did I do? I told him! I just blurted it out!"

"You did what you thought was right. You're not the one to blame here. He's the conniving bastard."

"And now the Order of Cotton Mather knows that I'm a witch." She turned to look at me. "They killed my father. They've killed so many of my people that I knew."

The mention of Gina's father brought back memories to me. Last winter, I'd worked on a case that involved Gina's late father—although it was hard to think of him as dead, as I'd had conversations with him. He hadn't exactly been a ghost, but he hadn't exactly been alive either. There was so much I didn't know about Gina's race. I knew their powers could extend beyond death, but I didn't know how.

One thing I did know, though, was that Gina's father, Eleazar, was one of the most powerful witches who had ever lived, and if he'd come back from the realm of the dead once, perhaps he could do so again. "Can he help?"

"My father? I don't think so. There are some rituals I can try, but… no, I don't think there's time."

"Other witches?"

"And risk exposing them to the Order?" Gina shook her head. "Too dangerous. Plus, they probably couldn't get here in time."

"Then we'll have to get you out of town. Get you somewhere safe."

She gave me an "are you insane?" look, one I was used to getting. "Where would I go?"

"It doesn't matter, as long as it's far away and you get away from these fanatics."

"But everything I love is here! You're here! Duncan, I can't leave you!"

"But if you stay—"

"Besides, you need me! That spirit that you're dealing with at Jason Church's house—"

"I'll deal with it. I can handle it on my own." We were getting good at interrupting each other, and I was shocked that I got to finish the sentence.

"You're doing a bang-up job of it so far!"

"He's a tricky one, I'll admit."

She was adamant. "I'm not going anywhere. You need me. Plus, I'll be miserable somewhere else."

"Tell that to the Indianapolis Tourism Board. They can adapt it as their slogan." I took in a deep breath and let it out slowly. "So you can't stay, and you won't leave."

"That's about the size of it."

"Which leaves us with Plan C."

"And what," Gina asked, "is Plan C?"

I told her. She listened. Several times she opened up her mouth to protest, but she heard me out. After I'd laid everything out, I said, "It means giving up a lot, for you, I mean. It's your decision."

She leaned forward, her elbows on her knees and her head supported by her hands, frowning. "I think we can do it. It would be a massive change, of course."

I nodded. "Yep."

"We'd need to—"

"Yeah. I already thought of that. Unpleasant." It was obvious which part of my plan she was questioning. "I can take care of that part. You'll have to work a lot of magic in between now and then."

"I can do that, no problem. But… this means a major change for us," she repeated.

"It's the only alternative that I can think of."

We probably would have spent the better part of the evening hashing out the details, but at that moment, my cell phone rang. It was Jason Church, and he sounded frantic. In fact, his first words were so garbled that I could make no sense out of them.

"Calm down," I said. "Tell me again. What's happened?"

"Anthony and Gary. They went to the house to get a few things, and they haven't come back. They've been gone hours now, and neither of them is answering their cell phones."

There was a lot I wanted to say, namely along the lines of asking Jason if his boyfriend had ever watched a horror movie, and didn't he know the one thing you *never* do is go back into the haunted house once you are safely out of it. Instead, I asked, "Where are you now?"

"I'm at Anthony's parents' house. What should I—" He choked on the rest of the sentence.

"Okay, you stay put. I'll go out to the house and see what's going on there. I'll find them. Don't worry." Easy words to say, but I knew how nasty old Doc Moore could get. Why, oh why, would Anthony go back there? And why would he take young Gary with him? If I found the two safe and unharmed, I knew it would take immense willpower not to kick Anthony in the nads for being so stupid.

Jason protested. "I want to come with you."

"That won't be happening. It's dangerous in that house. Apparently, I haven't made that clear enough."

"No, I have to go. I can't stay here, just waiting. I called you because I didn't want to go alone, but I have to go."

I pulled the phone away from my face so my growl didn't sound too loudly in his ears. After I'd gotten it off my chest, I returned the phone to speaking position. "Okay, meet me there in a half hour. Keep trying their cell phones." With luck, the two went to the house and got what they needed and left. The batteries of their cell phones could have drained while they were there. One liked to think optimistic thoughts.

After I'd hung up, Gina asked, "Want me to tag along?"

I shook my head. "No, you need to get working on your spells. I'm assuming this isn't shit you know off the top of your head and that you'll need to look some stuff up."

She scoffed. "These aren't your average spells and incantations we're planning. I'll have to do some heavy research."

"If," I said, rising from the couch, "you come across some spell in your research that will nobble Doc Moore for us, let me know."

"Nobble? Have you been reading Agatha Christie again?"

I just smiled at her, and somehow she managed to return the favor. I could see in her eyes, though, that despite the banter, she was sad. And why wouldn't she be? She'd just found out the guy she'd been dating was, for all intents and purposes, an enemy spy. Not only that, but a fanatical group of numbnuts was out to kill her. But that's what we did. We quipped through the pain. "You take care of yourself," I said seriously.

Gina nodded. "You too."

CHAPTER 9

I HAD been optimistic when I'd told Jason I'd meet him in half an hour. He didn't know that, in Duncan speak, half an hour really meant just over an hour, because first I had to stop by my place and get Robbie and Daisy. We were dealing with a multiple haunting, after all, and being dead himself, Robbie was our ace in the hole. Well, as long as we could keep Moore from zapping his energy. Daisy, I brought along on a hunch. For finding people in a hurry, Daisy couldn't be beat. She may have been a zombie, but her olfactory senses were still top-notch. I thought about calling Nick, but he was going to head to the library after he'd finished work, and I didn't want to interrupt his research. He might find something we could use. Especially as, so far, we were pretty much stymied at getting rid of Moore's ghost.

It was nearly eight o'clock by the time we pulled into the driveway of 175 Denmark Street. We parked behind Jason's Kia Rio, and he had been pacing back and forth the length of the car, waiting for us. When my headlights shone on him, he had his fingers up to his mouth, so I think some fingernail chewing had been going on as well. I shut off the car, and Daisy followed me out the driver's side. Robbie just went through the passenger-side door.

The night was chilly, if not downright cold. If it kept up like this, I'd have to hang up the leather jacket for the season and pull out the winter coat. The house was dark, but by the streetlight, I could see Jason was in a panic. He rushed up to me before I even got the door shut behind Daisy.

"Where have you been?" He rubbed a hand over his face. "God, I've been going out of my mind."

"You didn't go inside, did you?"

"No, you said…." He stopped as Daisy came up and sniffed his pant leg. "What's this?"

"That's Daisy."

"What's wrong with her? She looks… well, sick."

"She's had a cold." Well, it was better than telling him the truth.

Robbie was still standing by the side of the car. He was wearing a pair of jeans torn at the knees, a muscle T-shirt, and his high school letter jacket. He didn't feel the cold, but he knew it made me feel better when he appeared in weather-appropriate garb. He was gazing, not fondly, at the house.

"You can feel it, even out here," he said. Nodding toward a house across the street, he noted, "That house doesn't have any lights on, either, but it doesn't look as black as this one does. This one's darker than dark. Like its very soul is dark."

"That's Dr. Moore's soul, and once he's gone, the house will be just like the other Victorian monstrosities on this street." When Jason looked questioningly at me, I said, "Talking to Robbie."

"He's here?" You could tell by his tone Jason didn't really care one way or another. He just wanted to get in the house to see if his boyfriend and Gary were in there. Not waiting for an answer, he led the way to the front porch and was up the stairs, Daisy at his heels. Robbie and I took up the rear.

"Let me go in first," I said as Jason was inserting his key in the lock. "I want to get a feel for the Doc's mood before we all go traipsing through the place."

Robbie grimaced. "Like it's going to be anything but grumpy. How come we never get the cases where the ghosts like bunnies and go about singing Disney tunes?"

Jason stepped aside so I could enter. I tried the light switch, but of course it didn't work. The hairs on the back of my neck bristled, so the doctor was somewhere close. It felt like he was lurking in the background, watching us. And enjoying Jason's obvious distress.

I took a flashlight out of my jacket and was somewhat surprised that it worked. "Anthony?" I called out. There was no reply.

Behind me, Robbie and his cousin slowly entered. Jason gulped loudly. Even he could feel the electricity in the air. "Is he here?" he asked quietly.

I knew he was referring to his boyfriend, not the doctor. I played the beam around. Everything looked to be in place, and at least there were no smears of blood on the walls that I could see. "I don't know," I said. "Have you tried their cell phones lately?"

Jason nodded. "They still don't answer."

There was a coat closet to our left. I shone the flashlight at the doorknob. "Is there something of Anthony's in there? Something he's worn?"

"Sure." Jason moved past me and got out a gray hooded sweatshirt. "Will this do?"

"Perfect." I took the garment and got down so Daisy could sniff it. She didn't need coaxing, being an old hand at this sort of thing. She knew when I presented her with an unknown item of clothing that she was to go into hunting dog mode, and that's what she did. Once she had the scent, she was off as quick as her little legs would take her.

"He's here!" I said, taking off after her. Jason and Robbie followed. Daisy led us directly to the basement door. It was closed, so she stood in front of it, impatiently wagging her tail. She had to back up so I could open the door, but as soon as there was enough space for her to continue, she was through and could be heard thumping down the steps.

Anthony was there, right at the bottom of the stairs. His skin looked unearthly pale in the flashlight's glare, and the blood covering his face didn't help matters. He was lying in a fetal position. The blood was drying and had come from a gash on his forehead. There was a lot of it.

"Oh my God!" Seeing his unconscious lover, Jason pushed past me and rushed to his aid. "Anthony!" It could have been a trick of the light, but I though the injured young man's eyelids flickered a little at the sound of his name. Jason, tears in his eyes, grabbed Anthony's hand.

I got down on my haunches and did a quick check, setting the flashlight down close so we could still see. Daisy stayed by the bottom of the steps, knowing she'd done her job well.

The cut over his right eye seemed to be Anthony's only injury. His skin was cold to the touch, but it wasn't exactly balmy down in the basement. I took off my leather jacket and put it around him. "He's okay," I assured Jason. I took hold of Anthony's other hand and felt for a pulse. It was good and strong. "We need to get him to a hospital, though."

Jason fished out his phone with shaky fingers. He pushed a few buttons but then yelled out, "Fuck! There's no signal!"

"Okay. Go outside. You may have to get some distance from the house, but you'll get a signal out there. Robbie will stay here with Anthony. I'll look for Gary."

"Did he fall down the stairs?" Jason's voice was choked with emotion.

"I don't know. Maybe." Pushed was more likely, or, considering what had happened to Nick, he might have even taken the express route through the floor. "Go! Call!"

Jason nodded and hesitated only a moment. "I'll be right back, baby," he said, giving Anthony's hand a squeeze. Then he rose and noisily made his way up the stairs. He didn't have a flashlight with him, but I guess he knew the house well enough to make his way back to the front door without mishap. As long as he wasn't stopped on the way by a nasty spook.

When he was gone, Robbie got close to Anthony, taking up pretty much the same position Jason had. I picked up the flashlight and quickly checked the rest of the basement. No sign of Gary, so I started up the stairs. "Call me if you need me," I told Robbie.

"You be careful," he replied.

"Always." Daisy had, after Jason's departure, slowly crept closer to Anthony. I think the smell of the blood was too much for her, and she was licking her chops. Before she got too close, I called her sharply. "Daisy! You'd better come with me!"

She wasn't happy about it, but she trundled up the steps at my heels.

I went through the main floor, room by room, every now and then calling out Gary's name. There was no reply, just the soft padding of Daisy's paws on the carpeting. Time seemed to be standing still, and I had no idea how long I searched those rooms. There were goose bumps on my arms, and I could see my breath coming out in white puffs. I kept expecting to hear the wail of an ambulance siren, but none came. Maybe I hadn't been looking for Gary as long as I'd thought.

He was there, though. I felt it in my bones.

With a feeling of dread, I started up the stairs to the second floor. Daisy heard the sound before I did and growled as we both listened to a ghostly chuckle. It seemed to be coming from all around me.

"Fuck off," I told the disembodied laughter. It ceased, but I doubt if my cursing had anything to do with it. Old Doc Moore had made his point. He was in charge, and he knew it.

"Gary?" I called out for about the fifteenth time. Still no answer.

I got to the top step, and at first I started for the middle bedroom, but something drew me to the hall mirror. I turned to it, not knowing what to expect, only vaguely aware of Daisy sniffing at my heels.

I shone the flashlight beam across the glass. At first I saw nothing amiss, just my reflection and what little of the hall was illuminated behind me. Then there was a figure in the mirror transposed over mine. Gary was inside the mirror, pounding against the glass in terror. I couldn't hear either his cries for help or the thump of his hands against the mirror, but the poor kid was obviously beyond scared. Not that I blamed him. Seeing the young man there, frantically trying to make a sound or escape his predicament, my blood froze.

I got close to the glass. I had no idea if he could hear me or even see me, but I yelled, "We'll get you out. Don't worry!"

How, I didn't know. But I knew I would or die trying.

"HE'S *IN* the mirror?" Robbie asked.

"Yep."

Robbie shook his head. "I've been dead for more than ten years now, and I have no idea how you could do something like that."

"You don't have the twisted mind and the hatred that Dr. Moore has."

We were perched against the hood of my car. The EMTs had come and gone, carting along with them a semiconscious Anthony. One of the EMTs kept asking Anthony if he'd fallen down the stairs. The poor guy couldn't answer with more than a groan. Strangely—although, really, not so strangely—when the ambulance arrived, suddenly the house lights worked, and the atmosphere seemed normal. I wasn't really surprised by that. Moore was a bully, and while he didn't mind torturing Jason and his family, he didn't want to draw *too* much attention to himself. Not yet, at least. So when the EMTs burst in, it was just your normal old house on Denmark Street. They hadn't lingered. Once they had Anthony on a gurney and back up the stairs, they took off, asking Jason and me a few questions we couldn't answer. No, we didn't know what happened. We'd come in and found him at the bottom of the stairs. Jason had ridden with Anthony to the hospital in the ambulance. I promised I'd check on them later.

"Can we do anything for him?" Robbie asked.

I nodded with certainty. "Yeah. I don't know what, but yeah. We're going to help him."

"Should we just… I don't know… break the mirror?"

Sighing, I took out my cell phone. "I wish I knew. That might work, or it might be disastrous. Let me see what Gina says."

A quick call told us we shouldn't do anything so drastic. "Breaking the mirror could kill the boy," Gina warned. "Let me consult some books. Call me back in about fifteen minutes."

I hung up and shivered, and not just from the chilled air. I gazed toward the front of the house. The doorway was totally hidden in shadows, but I could feel the evil spilling out through the cracks.

We were quiet for about a minute. Robbie fidgeted a little. Daisy had found a spot on the grass and was curled up for a rest. Even she, though, kept a bloodshot eye on the dark edifice before us.

Finally, Robbie asked, "Should we go back inside?"

"Why? Until we have some way to nobble Dr. Moore, we're just exposing ourselves to danger. I don't want to take a chance on him zapping you," I said as I patted my ribs, "and as I'm almost totally healed now, I'm not wanting another sail through the air just yet. Honestly, you see people in movies go flying all the time, and the worst damage they get is mussed-up hair. Me, cracked ribs."

"How's Gina doing?" he asked.

I shrugged. "Under the circumstances, good. I mean, she just found out the guy she's dating wants her burned at the stake." I had already filled Robbie in on Mark and the Order of Cotton Mather. "That's enough to shake your belief that the world's a nice place to live in."

Robbie snorted. "If I was her, I'd be cursing his ass. Couple of boils on his butt. Warts on his nose. Penis falling off. That sort of thing."

"I probably would too. But Gina's not like that. She wouldn't harm anyone." I sighed heavily. "Which, if only those idiot cult members would see it, is exactly why they shouldn't be after her. Assholes." I checked the time on my cell phone. Still too early to call Gina back.

"What's she going to do?"

"She's got some spells going. Sort of an early warning system. If anyone comes onto her property, she'll know right away." And, if we could work it, we had Plan C. But I didn't feel like telling Robbie about that at the moment. He'd have lots of questions, which was understandable—hell, I had a bunch myself—but we had more immediate things to worry about, such as a fourteen-year-old *inside* a mirror.

"You're worried about her, aren't you?"

"Yep." I turned my head to look at him. Robbie was solid enough, but with only the lights from the street and neighboring houses to go by, he almost could have been a character from a black-and-white movie who had decided to walk off the screen. The only real color discernable was the brown of his eyes.

He gave me an encouraging smile. "She'll be okay. She's the most resourceful witch we know."

"She's the only witch we know, unless you want to count Eleazar. And he's dead." I frowned. "Sort of."

A light upstairs in the house next door went off, casting even more gloom over us. It felt like the whole street was giving the day up and going to sleep. There wasn't even much traffic, although you could hear the sound of cars heading down streets blocks away. Except for those travelers—most likely young people going to or coming from local bars—it seemed like Robbie and I were the last people still up.

Just to prove me wrong, the sounds of laughter came from a house down the street. Someone was having a party. Lucky them.

I was just about to phone Gina again when Robbie blurted out, "I heard you earlier. When you were talking to Gina. About when I move on."

"Oh?" I said, trying to sound noncommittal.

Robbie's smile turned to a wry one. "Yeah. You knew I was listening, didn't you?"

"Yeah." There didn't seem to be any point in lying about it. "Doesn't change anything, though. What I said was the truth."

"But you could have a real life!"

"Got one now."

He chortled and leaned against me. I couldn't feel much, of course, other than my right side getting cold as shit, but it was a nice gesture. I was feeling closer to him than I had in ages, and that was saying a lot. "There's the whole no sex thing."

"I've learned to live with it."

"But you don't have to. Without me around, you'd—"

"I'd be miserable." I reached over and took his right hand in mine. I could nearly feel it. "And that's okay too. I know you want to move on, and I won't stop you. But you seem to have the idea that if you do, everything will be hunky-dory for me, and I just needed to find a way to let you know that isn't the case. It wasn't right, me saying those things to Gina when I knew you could hear them. But sometimes it's hard to get you to listen."

"That's the pot calling the kettle black," Robbie said without bitterness. "You deserve to have a good life, though, Duncan. You deserve to have someone you can hold, make love to."

"I meant what I said. It wouldn't work. Not in the long run."

"But when you met Nick—"

I shook my head. "Yeah, I know. I thought I needed physical contact. And I won't lie to you. I have strong feelings for Nick. I like him a lot. But when it comes right down to it, it's just that. I like him. I love you. Always have, always will."

Robbie's face grew serious. Just about as serious as I'd ever seen him. "Then I'm not going."

My heart wanted to do a little dance of joy, but I commanded it to wait a moment. "Don't speak too hastily. You've said yourself that you feel drawn to the other side, that you should cross over."

Robbie pondered that a moment. "True. And I do feel, part of me, that I shouldn't be here. But I also feel like I should be. I know, it doesn't make sense."

"Sadly, it does. I'm feeling the same sort of emotions."

He leaned his head against my shoulder. "So what do we do? We seem to waffle between me going or not going. Well, okay, I waffle." He blinked. "I miss waffles. With blueberry syrup. Those things are the bomb."

"Yeah," I agreed, "we do seem lately to go between 'let's end this' and 'let's keep it going.' And I've put a lot of thought into this. I think it's because we've never made a formal commitment."

Robbie frowned. "What do you mean?"

"I mean that, this time, we make a promise to each other. If you're going to stay, you stay. No more talk of moving on. If you stay, it's for the duration." I smiled. "I'd say until death do us part, but that didn't even stop us."

Robbie, grinning like a kid at Christmas, lifted his head off my shoulder. He reached out his hand to guide my chin to bring my face close to his. He kissed me gently. I almost didn't even notice the cold. The gesture was enough to make the blood surge through my veins. There was enough actual contact that I could tell that he was still smiling through the kiss.

"I love you," he said.

I brought one of my legs up onto the hood of the car and shifted awkwardly, the leg now under me, so our bodies were facing each other as well. "And I love you. Always have. But in our situation, that doesn't seem to be enough. It's been hard on both of us. There's the whole no sex thing, the pull you feel to cross over, and my being in contact with living, breathing men who I can actually touch and feel and drive me crazy. So, like I said, a formal commitment is in order."

Robbie looked dubious. "Uh… hate to tell you this, Dunc, but gay marriage isn't legal yet in Indiana. And even if it were, I'm pretty sure that if you tried to get a marriage license for one living gay guy and one dead gay guy, they'd lock you up and conveniently forget where they put the key."

"I didn't say it would be legal." I took both his hands in mine. Sort of. As well as I could. "Robert Randall Church, do you promise to stay with me, to love me, and to be with me until my death puts us both on the same playing field?"

His eyes were glittering. "I do. And do you, Duncan Allen Andrews, promise to be with me always, to cherish me—because, let's face it, I'm worth a little cherishing—and to stop being so fucking hard on yourself?"

"I—wait, what was that last part?"

"Say I do, dumbass."

I nodded. "I do."

He cocked an eye at me. "No more fretting over my being forever twenty while you get those marvelous gray hairs and crow's feet around your eyes?"

"I don't have crow's feet."

"Not yet, you haven't."

I nodded again. "No more. And no more listening to paranormal jerks on TV like Ricky Vallis who say you should cross over."

"Cross my heart."

Our lips met again. The kiss was longer this time, and I tried not to think that I was really just pushing my lips into cold air. No, I was kissing my lover, in the best way we could. It would have to be enough.

The kiss might have gone on for ages if my cell phone hadn't interrupted. I was half tempted to ignore it, but I knew it would be Gina, and we did have business to attend to. I answered. "Yo."

"Okay," Gina said, "we've got something, I think. Nick's here with me. He's got some news, and I think I've found a spell that will put the kibosh on your angry ghostie."

"Kibosh? Who have you been reading?"

She ignored my query. "Meet us at your place."

"We can be there in twenty minutes."

"Twenty real minutes or Duncan minutes?"

Ouch. "Real ones." I hung up and told Robbie, "Time to roll." I called to Daisy, who had moved from her spot and was sniffing the ground, possibly to find the scent of something she could bite the head off of. Reluctantly, she returned to the car. As we settled in our respective seats and I was putting on my seat belt, Robbie, a grin plastered on his face, said, "I knew you'd come up with something."

"About?"

"Me moving on. I knew you'd come up with some plot or reason for me to stay." He scrunched up his lips. "I just wasn't sure what it would be. I gave you plenty of time. I mean, you had until New Year's."

"Have you been playing me?" I asked with a laugh. Surely not. I had been the one playing him, getting him around to my way of thinking. Had to be that way. Didn't it?

Robbie's grin grew until it threatened to burst off his face. "Now, would someone as sweet as me be that devious?"

I wished I knew.

CHAPTER 10

"I'VE BEEN going over the old newspaper accounts about Dr. Moore's death at the library," Nick said. He looked excited but tired. There were dark circles under his eyes from poring over old records, but also a tiny gleam of triumph. He tapped the cover of a library book on the table in front of him. "I also found a book on serial killers that had a chapter on Dr. Moore. It didn't really give me more info, nothing we didn't already know, although it did go into grisly detail. However, it did mention that the good doctor kept a journal."

"Nice of him," I said.

"Turns out the journal is in the special records section of the downtown library. You can't check it out, of course, but they do let you look at it. I made a lot of notes." To show he had, Nick flipped over several pages of the legal pad next to the serial killer book to show that pages and pages were filled with his neat handwriting. "Then I hit the old newspaper archives. One very interesting one. I made a copy."

We were seated around my dining table, with Nick opposite me. Gina had already seen the article in question, so he shoved the paper over to me. Robbie stood behind me, looking over my shoulder.

The headline read: "HEADLESS BODY FOUND IN BASEMENT." I skimmed the article. It had been written the day after Dr. Moore's death, and the details of his nefarious life hadn't yet come to light. The reporter had played up the horrific nature of the crime, and there was an underlying "Oh, how can someone have beheaded such a pillar of the community" suggestion in the writing. Days later, when the bodies of Moore's victims were discovered, the old coot wouldn't be considered such a pillar.

"His head was never found," Nick said. "I checked. He was buried sans noggin."

"So," I said slowly, "his head could still be there. Somewhere on the property."

Nick shrugged. "The police made a thorough search, but it was never located. The guy who wrote this book," Nick said, tapping the cover again, "speculates that, perhaps, the members of Moore's coven found his body before the police got there and made off with his head."

"If it's still around, that could account for some of Moore's extraordinary power. We'll have to locate it if we can." I rubbed a hand over my weary eyes. I hadn't yet apprised Gina and Nick of the events of the evening. "But, right now, we've got a more pressing problem."

I gave them the *Reader's Digest* condensed version of the night. They were both alarmed, but Nick was particularly aghast.

"You mean," he said, eyes wide, "that the kid is *in* the mirror?"

"Yep."

Nick looked from me to Gina and then back to me. "Can he do that? I mean, how do you put someone inside a mirror? Can he breathe in there? Is he alright?"

Gina answered. "It's possible, but it's pretty advanced magic. Which means that Moore was really good at black magic."

"We can get him out, though, right?" Nick addressed his question to me, but I let Gina answer. Magic was her area of expertise. Mine was being an asshole and shooting guys.

"I'm sure we can." Gina's voice was reassuring, and while her words didn't erase the worry from Nick's face, they did allow him to sit back in his seat and not look like he was going to explode. "Moore must have used a binding spell, confining Gary to the mirror. I can reverse it."

Nick pushed his papers and books out of the way. Moments before, he'd been so proud of his research, but now it obviously wasn't as important as Gary's predicament. "Then let's get going!"

Gina shook her head. "Not so fast. Duncan looks like he could use a couple of hours of sleep, and I have to get some things from my house.

It would also help if I had something of Gary's to use. Something organic would be best. A fingernail clipping or a lock of his hair."

"Where the hell are we going to get something like that?"

"Why don't you check with Jason," she said. "He might have some ideas. Even an article of clothing recently worn will do. Something that hasn't gone through the laundry yet. It will still have his essence and maybe even have a fallen hair or two."

"He'll still be at the hospital with Anthony," I added. To Gina, I said, "I'll go with you to get your stuff."

"Nonsense. You look exhausted. You need some rest. Grab a few hours of shuteye, and we'll meet back up and head out to the house." She smiled at Nick. "Don't worry. We'll have Gary out of there soon."

Nick wasn't entirely reassured. "Shouldn't we go out there now? I mean, the poor kid—"

"Rushing out there won't help him," Gina said. "We'll get him out as soon as possible."

I shook my head. "I don't like the idea of you going to your house alone."

"I'll be fine." Gina leaned forward and touched my arm. "Really. Get some rest. We'll be back here soon, and then we can rescue that poor boy. I'll rush in and get what I need and rush back out."

"At least take Robbie with you. If any members of the Order of Cotton Mather are about, he can appear and scare the bejesus out of them. If they can't see ghosts, then he can bean them with a brick."

Robbie nodded. "I can do that."

Nick blinked. "What's this Order of Cotton Mather?"

"I'll explain later." I felt good saying that. The heroes on TV are always telling their friends that. Of course, by not taking the time to explain, they inevitably put said friends in horrible danger. I opened my mouth to spout a quick rundown of what Mark the Dentist had been up to but then decided against it. It really would have to wait. "Just make sure Gina's safe. Don't let any strangers get near her."

Gina began to protest. "Really, it isn't necessary. I can—"

"He goes with you," I insisted.

"If," Gina said, relenting, "you promise to get some rest."

I promised, but only because my eyes were telling me they'd like a brief vacation from having to work. My brain was in full agreement, so I said, "I just need a quick nap."

Robbie smiled. "Enjoy your snoring."

"I don't snore."

He pursed his lips. "No. Of course you don't." He winked at Nick. "He snores like a band saw on overdrive."

WHEN EVERYONE had gone, leaving me with Daisy and droopy eyelids, I found myself hesitating. I was weary, that wasn't in question. A quick nap, and I'd be up for rescuing teenagers from mirrors until sunrise. Still, the idea of closing my eyes and letting consciousness go didn't appeal to me.

For weeks, I'd been having disturbing dreams. Not long before, I'd had a vision/dream in which I'd hunted Robbie down in the woods and shot him. In the dream, he'd been flesh and blood, and therefore, shooting him had consequences. True, the first time I'd had the nightmare, I'd been under the thrall of a vampire, and there was little doubt in my mind the vampire in question was using my memories to toy with me. Still, there must have been something to the dream, as I'd had it several times, even after said vamp had been turned to dust. I didn't relish the thought of having it again.

I picked up Daisy and headed over to the couch. I didn't want to snooze in my bed—too comfortable. I might want more than just a catnap there. No, the couch would do. And maybe—hopefully—I'd slumber peacefully.

I started off splayed lazily on the couch, with Daisy at my side, but soon I shifted until I was fully stretched out with the dog at my feet. In seconds, I could feel sleep taking over me, even as my head was going through plans.

I need to see Elton the Demon tomorrow, I told myself. *After getting Gary out, of course.*

And Gina. Nick. Robbie and I hadn't told them our news. The timing hadn't been right. Tomorrow, when things were calmer, I'd let them know Robbie had decided to stay with me. I smiled sleepily. Assuming Robbie wasn't spilling the beans to Gina right now. That would be like him. He had a hard time containing himself sometimes.

Don't have the dream.

Somehow, as I settled my head more comfortably against the couch pillow, I knew I wouldn't. I felt at peace. And in my last moment of wakefulness, I knew the dream didn't mean what I thought it had. I knew it with certainty.

I wasn't killing Robbie. I was killing the idea, long nestled in my subconscious, that I was hoping somehow he'd come back to life. I was killing the living *Robbie. Dominic Hunt, the vampire, found that thought in my brain and twisted it to his own purposes.*

Sleep came over me.

I DREAMED. *I wasn't in a wood hunting my lover, though. That was good. I was in a cave. No, it was a catacomb. There were niches along the wall in the corridor I was in. Some of them held caskets, some just skeletons exposed to the elements. I could hear the screeching of rats.*

I was walking. I knew where I was headed. I held an old-fashioned lantern in my hands. Its light was throwing eerie shadows all around me. When you're walking through a catacomb with bodies on either side of you, you really didn't need the added eerie shadows.

Ahead of me was a light. I walked slowly, and it seemed like I'd never reach it. In that weird way that dreams work, though, suddenly I came to a vast cavern, even though it seemed that moments before I'd had hundreds and hundreds of yards to go. The dream equivalent, it seemed, of a movie jump cut.

The cavern was illuminated by dozens of candles placed in niches in the walls. In the center of the room was a long wooden table. The chairs around the table had all been pushed back as if an important meeting had ended only moments before, and the participants had left in a hurry. There was one person in the room besides me, and he was seated at the far end of the table. A red candle burned in a silver holder on the table before him.

The man was wearing a simple black robe, and I recognized him immediately. Eleazar, Gina's father.

I wondered if I was having some sort of vision or if I was just having a regular dream.

"Does it matter?" Eleazar asked, as if reading my thoughts.

My dream self shrugged. "Well, if it's just a dream, I can sit back and just let it go. If you're trying to contact me in some way, I need to pay attention."

"Then," he said, "pay attention."

It would have been hard not to, in either case. Eleazar had one of those deep, commanding voices. No wonder he had been one of the most powerful witches who had ever lived. With a voice like that, a spell would have to sit up and take notice. You wouldn't dare to not meet up to Eleazar's expectations.

I approached the table.

"Sit," he told me. I sat. He leaned forward in his chair, studying me carefully. The room got brighter so he didn't have to squint, the candle flames dancing. "My daughter is in danger."

"I know. I'm going to protect her."

"I have no doubt," he said, his eyes troubled, "that you will try. There were those who said they could protect me, but the Order destroyed me in the end."

Not that it seemed to have put an end to his power. I didn't voice that thought, although Eleazar might have known what I was thinking anyway. Instead, I said, "I have a plan. I wanted her to leave town, but she wouldn't."

Eleazar grunted. "She is my daughter. She has my stubbornness. It could be the death of her."

"My plan needs time, though. Plus the help of a demon I call Elton."

He listened carefully as I explained my idea to him. I couldn't help but notice his frown deepened as I spoke. I got the feeling he wasn't overjoyed at my little plot. When I'd finished, he eyed me carefully.

"An audacious plan."

"Best I could think of."

He nodded. "I wish I could help you. My hands, in this matter, are tied." He indicated the empty seats. "The Council has forbidden me to act."

Council? The room did seem like it had, just moments before I'd entered, been filled. Even in death, did witches have a council that could help the living world? And why wouldn't they allow Eleazar to assist Gina?

"I see you have many questions," Eleazar said, a tiny smile on his lips. "I think, though, that the less you know of my people, the better. Gina trusts you, so I do as well. But mankind has hunted us for millennia. Many on the Council feel you already know too much about our kind."

"Nuts," I said, the word escaping my mouth before I remembered I was chatting with a powerful witch. "Sorry, but Gina's my friend. I'm not going to let anything happen to her, but the more I know—"

Eleazar held up a hand. "You don't have to convince me, young Andrews." He seemed to ponder a thought for a moment before he went on. "There is something I can do. It won't be directly helping Gina, so the Council won't object if they learn of my assistance."

He told me how he could help. When he finished, all I could say was "Holy shit."

The witch smiled. "Indeed," he said.

"You can do that?"

"I can," The word "easily" was implied. "But even my help may come to naught if the Order acts before you're ready."

"Oh, I'll be ready."

"I trust you're right." The room began to dim as a few of the candles were extinguished by a phantom breeze. *"Go now. And good luck."* As he spoke, Eleazar became enveloped in shadows. When the last word left his lips, he was no longer sitting at the table.

I awoke with a start. The sudden movement of my head coming off the cushion alarmed Daisy, who had been peacefully curled at my feet. Once she saw there was no immediate danger, she lowered her head and snuffed at me, as if angry I had disturbed her snooze.

"I miss the days," I told her, "when the worst dreams I had were showing up at school naked."

CHAPTER 11

"HE'S HERE," Gina said, her hands on the surface of the mirror. "I can feel him. He's very weak, but he's alive."

"The question is, can we get him out?" I was standing next to Gina, gazing intently into the mirror. It just looked like a regular refection to me, showing Robbie behind the two of us. Daisy was with us as well, but was too low to show in the mirror. Nick had wanted to come, but this time I insisted he get some rest. Plus, I didn't want to have to worry about Moore showing up and tossing him against a wall or having his minions try to pull him through the floor. I got paid for this shit. Nick didn't. Not that I'd charge Jason, of course. He was, in a way, family.

I glanced at Gina, wondering if she could sense I'd had contact with her father. I hadn't said anything about my vision. Somehow, I knew Eleazar didn't want her to know. Still, there was little I could keep from Gina. If she had any inkling, though, it didn't show in her face.

Behind us, Robbie was fingering the medallion hanging from a ribbon around his neck. Gina had given it to him, a charm to hopefully keep Dr. Moore from zapping Robbie's psychic energy. "He knows we're here," Robbie warned. "He's coming."

"Then we don't have much time," Gina said.

"Anything I can do to help?" I asked.

She shook her head. "Just hand me the shirt."

Nick had convinced Jason to leave the hospital long enough to go to Anthony's parents' to get one of Gary's shirts out of the dirty laundry. Gina thought it would do. It was a black T-shirt from a Foo Fighters concert that had been rescued from the clothes hamper. I didn't know how many days the kid had worn it in a row or what activities he'd been engaged in while wearing it, but it stank. If anything had Gary's "essence," it was this shirt.

She held the shirt in her left hand. Her right was pressed against the mirror. "Gary Anderson," she intoned. "I ask you to come forward. You are safe. We're here to help you, but you must come forward. Let us see you!"

"He's here. Moore's here," Robbie said, although the warning was unnecessary. The hairs on the back of my neck were doing a polka, and the hallway was suddenly cold enough we could see our breath. I nodded and picked up the shotgun I had placed on the hall table.

"Come forward, Gary," Gina continued. "I know you're frightened, but you're safe now. We're here for you."

The reflection in the mirror seemed to ripple, and then we could see Gary's face, superimposed over our own. His hair was matted as if he was swimming in something thick, and his eyes had dark circles under them. The kid looked pale and sick, and while he was still scared, you could see part of him was resigned to his fate and that he thought he'd be a prisoner of Dr. Moore's throughout eternity. Slowly, he raised a hand and placed it on the glass, right where Gina's was.

"Close your eyes, Gary," she said. "You can feel my hand, can't you? You can feel my fingers next to your own. Feel the warmth of my palm. You can—"

Gina went on, but I was only partially aware she was still speaking. Footsteps were coming up the stairs, loud, booming steps that shook the walls and made the chandelier over the foyer sway. There wasn't much light, but I could make out a shadow coming toward us. The doctor had arrived.

I cocked the shotgun and aimed, but before I could pull the trigger, the hall table shot out from its spot against the wall and rammed into the back of my legs, sending me sprawling. I went backward over the table and flipped over before hitting the floor. The gun went flying from my grasp. I hit my head on the wall as I landed and winced as the pain shot through my head. The hall seemed to get darker—which I wouldn't have thought possible—and I hoped it was an actual occurrence and that I wasn't in danger of blacking out from the head trauma. Robbie and I had to give Gina time to work her magic.

I sensed more than saw Moore coming closer to me. My eyes weren't focusing properly, although they were trying their best, and all I knew was that something big and black was now only a few feet from where I lay in a heap. I tried to sit up, but my head protested in no uncertain terms.

My eyes finally decided to work again, and I saw the ghost of Dr. Moore standing over me. With a wicked grin on his face, he bent down with his hands reaching out for my throat. I growled through the pain and brought my hands up to protect myself, but I wasn't moving fast enough.

"Come through the mirror, Gary!" I could hear Gina saying as Moore's fingers closed around my throat.

"Oh no you don't, fucker!" I heard Robbie shouting.

There was a flurry of movement in front of me, and suddenly the ghost's hands were away from my neck as Robbie hit Moore in the side with a flying tackle. Moore snarled and vanished as soon as Robbie's body collided with his, which was a good thing for my throat but not so great for Robbie, whose momentum kept him going. He would have hit the wall had he been corporeal, but he went partially through it instead. He recovered quickly, yanking his side out of the unblemished plaster with ease, and turned to see if I was okay.

"I'm fine," I said. I wasn't, but one always lied in these situations. "How's Gina—"

I didn't have to finish. I managed to sit up, and I could see Gina had succeeded. She was kneeling over the recumbent figure of Gary. Even in the dim light, I could see he was slick with sweat and breathing heavily like he'd just been through a battle. Which he had.

"He's okay," Gina told us. "He's very weak, but he's okay. You'll have to help me get him downstairs, though."

And who, I wondered, was going to help me? I bit my lip and tried to stand. I made it on the second try, and although my head felt like someone had built a bonfire in my cranium, I found I could function reasonably well. Gina and I got the kid up, and holding him between us, we got him down the stairs, Robbie following behind. Upon our arrival, we'd left the front door open, figuring the lights wouldn't work and it might allow a little more light inside so we could see a little. That and it made a hasty retreat easier if we had to make one.

The door slammed shut right before we got to it. Gina reached out with her free hand and tried the knob. "Locked," she said.

My shotgun was still upstairs, and as it was loaded with rock salt, it wouldn't have been much good for blasting the lock anyway. I thought about trying to kick it open, but that worked much better in movies than in real life. Besides, my head was throbbing and wouldn't take well to my body throwing itself against a thick door. Instead, I looked at Robbie.

He nodded, knowing what I wanted him to do. He shoved his hand into the metal plate surrounding the doorknob and began to feel around for the locking mechanism. Soon there was a satisfying click, and Robbie turned to us with a triumphant grin.

We bundled Gary out onto the porch, and as we crossed the threshold, I could hear a low voice coming from the stairway behind us.

"You will all die!"

As Gina and I were supporting the kid, Robbie closed the door behind us. I could tell it took one hell of an effort on his part, but he did it. His tackle upstairs had already used up most of his mojo. "Not today, thank you," he replied.

ELTON THE Demon leaned back in his rickety chair, counting the money I'd just handed him. His lip twitched when he got to the end. "There's more here than we agreed on."

"A bonus. For going above and beyond the call of duty."

He nodded and set the bills down in a neat stack in front of him on the desk. He eyed me carefully. "You look tired."

"Had a tough night and only a little sleep."

He scratched his cheek with one of his thick, meaty fingers. I noticed the fingernail was yellow and overly long. Well, on a human, it would have been. Apparently having satisfied his itch, he then put his hand almost lovingly on the bundle of money. "For a human, you're not so bad, Andrews."

"And you're a prince among demons."

Elton made a sound I think was a laugh. Maybe he had a chicken bone stuck in his throat. With demons, it's hard to tell. "Anything else I can do for you?"

"Leave town and never come back."

"Planning on it," he said. He added, "Not all demons are horrible monsters, you know. Some of us strive to live good lives."

"Yeah? How many people have you killed this week?"

"Two." He said it like it was a ridiculously low number. "One was a homeless person, so he won't even be missed."

"And that makes it all right?"

Elton continued as if I hadn't interjected. "The other was a mean-spirited fat man who was a terror to his family. I did them a favor by devouring him." He closed his eyes, smiling gently. "He was tasty."

I sighed and stood up, giving one last longing look at the pile of money Elton had his hairy mitt on. My bank account had said ouch when I'd taken out the money, and there was a little niggle in my brain that said I should just kill Elton and take the money. A deal, however, was a deal. And I had to admit Elton had come through with flying colors. "If anyone asks," I said, "you and I are mortal enemies, and we were here fighting and trying to kill each other."

He snorted. "You think I want it to get around that I was making deals with a mortal? And a known demon killer like yourself?"

I walked toward the warehouse door. I didn't turn, but waved a hand in farewell. "Thanks."

"You're welcome. And I hope your witch survives this."

I had my hand on the doorknob. "She will."

I WASN'T overly fond of hospitals.

Not that many people are, except for those who work there. But after seeing Elton the Demon and then making a quick trip to Gina's cottage, I felt I should check in at Wishard Memorial Hospital to see how Gary was doing.

I found Jason, Gina, and Nick in a little waiting room on the second floor. The moment I entered, Gina rose from the uncomfortable-looking chair she'd been in. Nick and Jason had it better, a padded two-seater that looked only marginally more comfortable. Gina hugged me.

There was also the ghost of a young woman sitting near the television set, which had some talk show on. She was sickly looking, and I wondered if she'd recently passed away in the hospital and hadn't realized she was dead yet. Maybe when he had some spare time, Nick could talk with her and see if she wanted to move on. At the moment, he seemed unwilling to leave Jason's side. The poor guy was clearly overwrought. He barely lifted his head when I came in the room.

"Gary's going to be okay," Gina informed me. "He's severely dehydrated, but other than that, there seem to be no physical symptoms. He's still in shock, but the doctors say he's improving moment by moment."

"And Anthony?"

"Still being held for observation, but basically recovered. They told Jason he'd be released later this afternoon."

Whenever you go to a hospital with head trauma, they hold you for at least twenty-four hours for observation, something I'd learned over and over again in my job. Often, after being conked on the head, I'd been carted off to the nearest hospital before I knew what was happening due to some well-meaning soul having called 911 after witnessing the incident. I could hardly say, "No, it's not necessary. My best friend is a healing witch. She can take care of me." Say something like that, and they keep you for much longer than twenty-four hours.

Jason let out a weary sigh and slowly stood. "I'm going to see if I can find someone who can give us an update. Then I'm going to Anthony's room." He smiled weakly at me. "He was sleeping earlier, but he should be up by now."

Nick had been sitting with his head in his hands. He sat up, looking first at the woman's ghost and then at Jason. "Want me to come with you?"

Shaking his head, Jason said, "I'm fine. Thanks for being here, though."

Jason paused as he passed us, walking to the doorway. He looked like he wanted to say something, but he didn't have the words. I touched his shoulder.

"This ends tonight," I told him. "I promise. You'll have your house back."

He let out a short, mirthless laugh. "After all this, I'm not sure that I want it back."

I watched him leave the room and turn down the hall. I couldn't blame him. I knew he'd been through a lot, but I hoped once the house was clear, he'd change his mind. Maybe if they got rid of all of Jason's aunt's stuff—especially that damned mirror—and started fresh, things would be different. Eventually, the bad memories would fade. I hated to see them give up a great old house like that.

But I was used to ghosts and dealing with nasty things. Maybe selling the house would be the best thing for them. In either case, though, I'd had it up to my neck with old Doc Moore and his antics. Tonight was his last night on this earth, that much I knew.

Gina brought me out of my reverie by saying, "I'm going to go get a coffee. You want anything?"

"I want tons of things. Somehow, I don't think the solutions to any of my problems are going to be in the hospital cafeteria, so I think I'll pass."

"Nick?" she asked.

"I'm fine." He answered so quickly, I wasn't sure the question had actually registered yet. It was a reflex response. When the words sank in, he added, "I'm not really a coffee drinker."

"Neither am I, but I'm thinking gin might be in short supply down there." Gina gave me a peck on the cheek. "Be right back."

Alone with Nick. Great. I had to tell him about the decision Robbie and I had made. He deserved to know. I mean, I knew how he felt about me. And I had strong feelings for him. But a newly committed Duncan and Robbie changed things. I had to let Nick know there wasn't a chance for the two of us. Let him off the hook.

I sat down next to him. Alone with Nick. Hell.

Well, if you didn't count the spirit sitting across from us. She had faded a little, but as I gazed across the room at her, she solidified somewhat. "Hi," I said.

"Hello," she replied meekly.

Nick filled me in. "Her name is Carla."

"Hey, Carla." Talking to a ghost was one way to stall for time so I could think of words to say to Nick.

"She doesn't know she's dead yet," Nick whispered.

Carla must have good hearing, though, because she shook her head. "I can't be dead. That's ridiculous."

I asked, "What's the last thing you remember, Carla?"

She frowned. "I was driving to work. I work at the Pottery Barn up in Castleton."

Ah. Auto accident. Must have been so quick she didn't even realize she was in an accident. "Nick's right. I'm afraid there was an accident."

The word accident seemed to trigger a memory. Her frown deepened.

"They brought you here to the hospital," Nick told her, "but it was too late."

Carla's eyes bore into Nick's face, searching for some sign he was joking with her. Seeing that he was serious, she said, "But I'm sitting here. I'm alive. I have to be."

"Your spirit hasn't realized that you've died yet." Nick was gentle but firm. "You can pass over to the other side if you want. You've got people waiting for you there."

"Close your eyes," I told her. "You'll see that he's speaking the truth. You'll know it. You can accept it and move on. If you stay here, you'll be able to see the ones you love who are still alive, but they won't be able to see you. It will be very lonely. If you allow yourself to go to the other side, you'll meet up with them again someday."

She closed her eyes, still shaking her head. Tears had begun to run down her cheeks. Just as a sob escaped her throat, a bright light began to surround her. It gained in intensity until Nick and I had to shield our eyes from it. Then the light was gone, and Carla's chair was empty.

Neither Nick nor I said anything for minutes after Carla's departure. My mind was racing, not only going over what we'd just done but also scrambling for something to tell Nick.

Finally, Nick said, "I wonder what heaven is really like. I mean, I told her that her loved ones were waiting, but I don't really know. That's just my belief."

"Sometimes belief is all you got to go on. Sometimes it's enough." Heaven. The decision Robbie and I had made would keep my boyfriend from going there. For now. But he'd get there eventually. With me by his side. That's the way we wanted it, and that's the way it was going to be.

Now I had to let Nick know. I opened my mouth to speak. I closed it again. "Nick," I said. Third attempt. Not bad.

"Yeah?"

I sighed deeply. "Nothing." Duncan, you chicken shit.

Nick slumped back in his seat, letting his legs splay out in front of him. He looked very tired. "It would be horrible, I think, to be a ghost and not be able to make yourself known to your husband, your wife, boyfriend, whatever. To watch them go on living, and not be able to interact with them. Robbie was lucky. You can see spirits. Most ghosts, from what I've seen, are lonely creatures."

Thanks for opening the door, Nick. He'd given me the perfect opportunity to let him know. *Speaking of Robbie....* Go ahead, Duncan. Tell him.

"Nick," I said.

"Yeah."

Again, the words failed to come. I just couldn't do it. The timing wasn't right. I'd tell him later, after we'd dealt with Doc Moore and Gina was out of danger from the Order of Cotton Mather. When things had settled down and we weren't running around like chickens with our heads cut off.

I got up. "I'm going to see if I can find Gina. She should have been back by now."

Nick nodded. "Oh, how are your ribs? I've been meaning to ask."

"Totally healed. Gina's methods work faster and better than anything they've got around here. Don't tell the doctors that, though. They'd be jealous."

I got to the door when Nick said, "Hey, if they've got hot chocolate or anything like that, get me one. I wouldn't mind a hot chocolate right now."

"Sure. Oh, and Robbie has decided to stay. We've decided to re-commit as a couple." The words just came out. I certainly hadn't meant to say them. It was one of those instances where the brain found the words and sent them straight through the mouth. Thinking wasn't really involved.

I wasn't facing Nick, but I could sense him freezing in place as my words sank in. "Oh," he said simply.

I was standing in the doorway, one foot out in the corridor and one still in the room. I ran a hand up and down the doorframe like it needed sanding or a good dusting. I watched the nurses working at their station a little ways down the hall. "Yeah," I said.

"I'm not surprised."

I turned to look at Nick. There was a smile on his face, one of those equal parts sad and happy smiles. "I couldn't let him go," I said. It sounded a bit like an apology, which I guess in a way it was.

"Of course you couldn't." Nick got up and came over to me. Embracing me in a tight hug, he said in my ear, "Anyone could see that you and Robbie love each other. You belong together."

"Thank you." He was holding me pretty tight, and I winced slightly as I spoke. Gina's magic had indeed healed my ribs, but they were still a little sore, and they protested at being treated like they were in a wrestling match with Hulk Hogan. Nick realized what he was doing and pulled back. His eyes were glistening and wet, but no tears were actually falling, which was good, because I didn't think I could have handled it. I felt bad enough for the guy as it was. I knew how he felt about me—he'd made that abundantly clear—and here I was letting him know he didn't have a shot, even a remote one. I was happy for me, but I felt like a cad. Sometimes when you get what you want you feel guilty, like you don't deserve the Big Happy.

To ease the tension, Nick punched me lightly on the arm. "I knew you guys would work it out."

"That's more than I did."

We stood there awkwardly. It seemed like one of us should say something, but for the life of me, I couldn't think of anything, so I repeated my last sentence, just adding a "yeah" at the beginning. I put my hands in my pockets and shuffled my feet a bit. Nick scratched the top of his head, then his cheek. After giving his cheek a good gouge, he found a spot on his neck that needed going over. One of us had to say something before he ran out of body parts to scratch.

"I thought…." Good start. What did I think? Apparently nothing, because after saying the words, nothing else followed.

"What?" Nick asked.

What I really wanted to ask was if we were still friends, but there wasn't a way to be that blunt. I wouldn't blame Nick if he didn't want to have anything further to do with me and my little band of crazies. After all, when we'd first met, he'd been living a normal life as a history teacher. Now, here he was, involved with demons, ghosts, witches, and other things that went bump in the night and sometimes attempted to gnaw your arm off. Gina had opened up his psy abilities so he could not only see ghosts, but communicate with them. His life would never be the same again. Sure, she could cloud that bit of his brain so the ghosties went away, but what would that do? He'd know they were there. He'd know vampires were real and there were creatures lurking down dark alleys, just waiting for the right moment to strike.

I'd put him through a lot, and in a way, I had strung him along emotionally as well. I'd never promised him that if Robbie went away there would be Nick and Duncan, living happily ever after, but there had been that possibility. And now I'd yanked that possibility away. I wouldn't blame Nick if he told me to fuck off and walked out of my life.

But I didn't want him to. I wanted him to stay my friend.

"I just…." Another good start. Maybe I should just speak the first two words of every sentence from now on. Just fill in the blanks, world. I pursed my lips in thought, feeling like an ass.

"So what do we do now?" Nick asked.

Good old Nick. With that simple little sentence, he let me know there was still a "we." He was still with us, me and the crazies. He was still part of us. "Now," I said, "we kick the ghost butt of one Doctor Stanley Moore."

CHAPTER 12

WE WERE having a council of war.

I even had handouts. I'd never had handouts before—it had never seemed necessary, but this time, I had handouts. I thought about going whole hog and putting all the pages together in neat little binders with everyone's name on theirs, but I decided that was going too far. So I just handed stapled-together sheets to Gina and Nick. Robbie had pages as well, but to save his energy, his weren't stapled. They were laid out in order on the table in front of his chair.

Gina and Nick sat opposite each other. I let Robbie have the chair at the head of the table, where I usually sat. I wasn't in a sitting mood. I wanted to pace.

"Okay," I said. "First, I want to thank Nick for his research. I had thought that this would be just a quick zap-a-ghost case, in and out, back in time for tea, but instead we find that a super ghost haunts 175 Denmark Street.

"Thanks to Nick," I went on, pausing briefly to give him a nod, "we know quite a bit about our spirit, and it's worth going over what we know of his life—and death—as any knowledge we have may come in handy when we head out to spank his behind."

"So we're on page two now?" Robbie asked. I'm pretty sure he was the class smartass when he was in school.

"Yeah."

"After 'Introductory Remarks by Duncan?'"

"Hey, if you don't like the handouts, I can just chatter and maybe leave out something important, and we end up with egg on our faces again tonight because of it."

Robbie shook his head. "No, I like the handouts. I especially like that you've prehighlighted certain sections. Lets me know what's likely to be on the quiz later."

When my pacing took me close enough to him, I tried to give Robbie a smack on the head. My hand went right through him, of course, but I think I got my point across. "If I may continue."

"Please do," Gina said. "Otherwise," she added, flipping to the last page, "we may never get to 'Finishing Remarks' and 'Time For Questions.'"

I knew they were just joshing me, but I still growled. "Try to do something nice for people, lay it all out nice and neat, and…."

"In fairness," Nick piped up, "the handouts were my idea. I guess it was the teacher in me."

"And if we're done with the teasing, I'll let Nick give us a quick biography of Dr. Moore."

Robbie frowned. "It's all written down here. We can just read it."

I gave him my sternest look, which was damned stern. It'd been known to silence crying babies, yapping dogs, and Jehovah's Witnesses wanting to give me leaflets.

"Or," a chastised Robbie said, "we can listen to Nick give us a quick biography of Dr. Moore."

"Well," Nick said, briefly checking his notes, "we know that Moore bought the house in 1923. He lived there by himself for the first year and a half. In January of 1925, he took in a teenager, Jeremy Kilgrove. Kilgrove was sixteen. Moore told neighbors that he was a nephew who was going to stay with him for a while.

"According to some sources, Kilgrove was the one that got Moore interested in black magic. The two of them started a coven, with some of their more disreputable neighbors joining them. It's not known exactly when Kilgrove was murdered, but he wasn't seen by anyone outside of the house after that summer. The book I read speculated that

Moore and the other members of the coven used Kilgrove as a blood sacrifice."

Gina asked, "Was Kilgrove mentioned much in Moore's diary?"

Nick shook his head. "He wrote quite a bit about the coven and the rituals they tried but rarely used names. Even the young men he took in were only referred to by their initials, if he mentioned them at all. Moore does state that he sometimes would bathe in the blood of his victims, thinking that it would give him supernatural powers."

"The same idea as eating the heart of your enemy," Gina said, nodding. "Moore wasn't far off. Under the right circumstances, one can gain power using blood or eating parts of the human body."

"Ick," Robbie muttered.

Nick glanced up at me. "Should I skip to the end?" Poor Nick. Robbie and Gina probably weren't any better audience members than his students.

I found pacing wasn't helping me to think, nor was it calming me down. I stood behind Robbie. I felt jittery and wanted desperately to chew my fingernails, but I had made a promise to myself to keep keratin out of my diet. "Okay, but we need to stress that Moore was a practitioner of the black arts, and each of his victims probably gave him more and more power. He still has power over those he murdered, if Nick's journey through the floorboards is anything to go by. Continue, Nick."

He cleared his throat first. "Toward the end of his life, things started going wrong for the doctor. His neighbors shunned him, thinking him a madman—"

"In fairness," Robbie chimed in, "he was."

Nick nodded in agreement. "Even members of his own coven began to fear Moore, and soon they stopped joining Moore for his rituals. Then we come to June of 1938, when neighbors informed the police that they had heard screams coming from the house. They investigated and found that Moore had stabbed his latest lover, Ben Turnbridge, to death, and then took his own life. However, Moore's head was missing. Apparently someone had severed his head in between the time Moore killed himself and the time the police arrived.

Some speculate that members of the coven had decapitated Moore, although no one knows for sure. The head was never found."

I smiled my thanks to Nick. "We'll assume the head is somewhere on the premises, only because Moore's power indicates that some part of him is in close proximity. Granted, it must be really well hidden, as no one's found it, and the house has been occupied in the intervening years. Floorboards, in the walls. It's there somewhere."

"And how are we going to locate it?" Nick asked.

"Daisy. Gina can help her out, giving her a magical nudge, enabling the dog to hone in on the skull. If it's there, Daisy will find it. Then we cleanse the damned thing with salt and torch the sucker."

Nick started to raise his hand for a question before realizing the movement wasn't necessary. To cover up, he changed the motion to a scratch of his chin. "Um, but don't we need to torch all his bones? There's the rest of his body, buried in—" He checked his notes. "—Washington Park East Cemetery."

"Already taken care of. Gina was there earlier, and she zapped the bones buried there." There hadn't even been all that much bother in digging up the grave, which was nice. She had merely intoned a spell over the plot, and poof! Bones be gone.

"Can't she just do that at the house?"

Gina answered, "I can, but I have to be close to the bones. Daisy will have to locate them first."

"Here's the plan for tonight," I said. "Nick, if you're game, you'll be with Daisy and find the skull. Robbie and I will keep Moore busy, so you shouldn't have to worry about him. Gina will also provide you with a charm that should help to ward off any of his ghostly helpers."

"Help?" Nick obviously wanted something more definite.

"Magic doesn't always work with spirits," Gina told him. "We'll just have to hope."

"You don't have to—" I started to say to Nick.

He stopped me. "No, I want to help. Really. I want to be there. After all, that bastard had his goons pull me through the floor. I hate to be vindictive, but I want to hear the bastard scream as we send him to hell."

"And that," I said, "brings us to our ace in the hole. Just in case torching Moore's bones doesn't do the trick—and it might not, since he's made that house a powerhouse of ghostly energy—Gina has a spell that should take care of him."

"I found a spell that will create a portal," she said. "We just form the portal around him, and it sends him to where he should be."

"Where he should be?" Robbie arched an eyebrow.

"The portal sends whomever steps through it to their final destination, or so the spell promises. If he's to go to hell, that's where he'll go."

Nick looked dubious. "I thought you just said magic doesn't work well with spirits. What if this doesn't?"

Gina smiled. "It will, because the spell doesn't directly affect him. I'll just be creating the portal. If I tried to use a spell on Moore himself, sending him to hell, it would likely fail. But I'll just be making a portal. The fact that he'll be inside it shouldn't matter."

"Shouldn't?" Nick didn't bother to disguise his worry.

I waved my hands. "It's okay. It's just Plan B. Just in case the torching of the skull doesn't finish Moore off. Which it will." I hoped I sounded more confident than I felt.

Robbie flicked his fingers, trying to shift the papers in front of him. The corner of one page actually lifted slightly off the table. "Was that," he asked with a smirk, "the 'Finishing Remarks?' Is it now time for questions?"

I shrugged. "Shoot."

"When are we doing this?"

"Tonight. We'll meet up around midnight and head over there."

Nick frowned. "Why so late? It seems like Super Ghost has more energy after the sun has gone down. We should go there now. You know. Attack him when he's napping."

I sighed as I flashed a sidelong glance at Gina. She was avoiding my gaze, concentrating on her handouts. "Gina," I explained, "has to have some time to work some spells. She's got a couple that she's got to use, and she needs some time."

"Well, we can—" Nick began.

I cut him off. "We're not going out there half-cocked."

"No, that wouldn't be fun at all," Robbie muttered. "Full-cocked or nothing."

"We wait until we have a full arsenal. I'm not having my ass handed to me this time by some ghost with an exaggerated sense of importance." I stood at the corner of the table and leaned against it, putting my palms flat on the surface. "Tonight, we roast the bugger."

It was meant to be a statement to rally the troops—well, the three of them—and fill them with confidence. The looks I saw around the table showed me I fell pretty far short of that.

"WE SHOULD get rings," Robbie said.

"You couldn't wear a ring," I replied.

"Gina can zap mine so I can wear it." He yanked the charm Gina had given him out from under his T-shirt and held it for me to see. Generally, ghosts could only appear in clothing or with accessories they'd worn in life. For instance, Robbie couldn't show up at a Halloween party dressed as a pirate, as he'd never worn pirate garb when he'd been alive and walking around. Which was a shame, because he'd make a good pirate.

We were walking through Castleton Square Mall and had just passed a jewelry store, which prompted Robbie's remark about rings. The mall was fairly crowded, and every now and then someone would walk past us, then pause and look back, wondering if they needed their eyes checked. Not many people could see ghosts clearly, but a few saw shadows or misty figures, and they probably weren't expecting to spot one sauntering by Abercrombie & Fitch. For someone like me, who could see them clearly, I was pleased to note few ghosts were hanging around the mall. There was one older lady who was haunting the JCPenney store, still working the cash register years after her death. I wondered if the management was pulling out their hair trying to figure out why phantom sales were being rung up.

I slowed my pace, thinking over Robbie's suggestion. "That's not a bad idea."

"Really?" Robbie tried to dodge out of the way of a mother with a toddler in a stroller. The mother, oblivious to his presence, walked right through him. The kid cooed, enjoying the experience of passing through a person—children three and under could usually see ghosts—but the mother's only reaction was to shiver a little.

"Yeah."

Robbie stopped dead in his tracks. "Can I get that in writing?"

I smiled and indicated the jewelry store we'd just passed. We'd come to the mall so I could get some grub. I hadn't felt like cooking. But a little ring shopping wouldn't hurt. "Let's check some out."

We spent several minutes peering into glass cases, finding several we both liked. With the clerk in close proximity, I couldn't say much aloud to Robbie without looking like a madman talking to himself, but he was used to my grunts that meant yes and the growls that meant no. Finally, we found two we both liked.

The clerk, a balding man in an ill-fitting suit, sensed he might have a sale and came closer. "Is there something I can show you, sir?"

I pointed. "I'd like to see this one, please."

He smiled that practiced smile salesmen who are on commission have down pat, the one that says, "Oh, you're so smart. That's an excellent choice." Aloud, the clerk said, "This is a very nice ring." He looked at it like he might start slobbering any moment. "A beautiful engagement ring. A band of white gold, and you've got round white diamonds surrounding the row of blue diamonds."

"I didn't know there were blue diamonds," I said.

"I think they dip them in Kool-Aid," Robbie joked.

The clerk's smile was now indulgent. "They're specially treated to make them permanently blue."

Robbie snorted. "Told ya."

I ignored him and asked the clerk, "How much is this little bauble?"

"$999.99."

"They really want to avoid using that 'thousand' word," Robbie said.

"A thousand bucks?" I tried not to choke on the words.

With a smirk, Robbie said, "I'm worth it."

"True," I replied.

The clerk couldn't figure out why I'd said true, but he wasn't about to let a sale slip through his fingers by questioning me over stray words. "Maybe you'd like to see some other rings, sir?"

A thousand bucks would put a serious dent in the bank balance, and I didn't have a paying case at the moment and none in sight. Still, Robbie and I had been through so much together. We deserved something nice. And it went nicely with the ring Robbie liked, a similar one without the blue diamonds. I shook my head. This was the ring. I just wasn't going to buy it right then and there.

The clerk expanded on his sales pitch, which wasn't really necessary, as I'd already made up my mind, but he seemed to like showing off his knowledge. We ended up with me saying I'd think about it and the clerk handing me his card. I assured him I'd be back to see him.

Robbie and I resumed our trek to the food court. "We should have had him show the ring I liked as well." Robbie was grinning from ear to ear, and there was a bounce in his step. "And you should have let him know that you were interested in getting the rings so you could wed your deceased boyfriend. Just so we could have seen his face."

I made sure Robbie could see my frown. "Wed? We talked commitment. We never said anything about getting hitched."

He looked hurt. "Well, I figured…. I know we can't legally get married, but I thought that was what you meant." He made a wry face. "Married in spirit, so to speak."

"In that case," I said as I got down on one knee.

Robbie had walked two paces before he realized I wasn't beside him any longer. He stared at me as I looked up at him. He wasn't the only one gaping at me. Several shoppers cast worried glances my way, wondering if I needed medical attention or if I was merely stopped in front of the toy store to tie my shoe and was taking my own sweet time about it. "What are you doing?" he asked.

"What do you think? I know we don't have rings yet, but that's coming. We'll have to get your ring size, and Gina can work her mojo so you can wear it. But in the meantime—"

"You're crazy," he said.

"Yep. But you already knew that."

"You're seriously going to propose to me in the middle of Castleton Square Mall?"

"A cemetery might be more appropriate—"

"Funny."

"So what do you say? Robbie Church, will you marry me?"

A trio of teenage black girls stopped when they heard my words. They giggled at the crazy guy on one knee proposing to thin air.

"Yes," Robbie said, "if it will get you up off the fucking floor. No one can see me, but I'm embarrassed just the same. Seriously, get up."

I laughed and got to my feet. I put a hand on his shoulder, and just for a second, we had contact. Then my hand went through him. "Unconventional, true, but we've hardly ever been conventional. Where are you going? The food court is this way."

Robbie, all grins, was jogging backwards. "I'm going back to JCPenney's to tell that ghost we saw there. I've got to tell somebody! You go on. Eat your food. I'm going to do some celebrating. Heck, I may even float around a bit."

His feet weren't touching ground as it was.

CHAPTER 13

I TOOK a sip and winced. I'd never been much of a coffee drinker—in fact, for most of my life, I'd shunned the beverage, thinking it tasted similar to mud mixed with water from a stream recently been visited by yaks with full bladders. Recently, though, I found that if I added enough milk and sugar, it was palatable. True, the amount of milk and sugar was on the heavy side, and one might argue it was closer to sugary milk with a little bit of coffee thrown into the mix, but to me, I'd become a coffee drinker. What had just gone down my throat, however, wasn't fit for human consumption. Maybe I was just shit at making coffee. I tossed the remainder of my mug into the kitchen sink.

The apartment was quiet. It was early evening but already dark outside. I hadn't bothered to switch on any lights, so I was surrounded by gloom. Robbie was resting, saving his energy for our encounter with Moore's ghost. Nick was at his place, catching a few Zs. Daisy was doing the same, only she was snuggled on our couch. Her toy squirrel, which had been well chewed, was beside her. Gina was at her cottage, probably stirring a bubbling cauldron and muttering about oil and trouble or whatever the spells she needed to cast called for. Okay, the bubbling cauldron was unlikely. But I'd be willing to bet the next month's rent that she had enough candles lit to keep the people at Yankee Candle happy for days.

I walked quietly into the living room. Daisy was snoring loudly. Gina had already planted the thought into the dog's head that she was to find a human skull, and the pooch seemed to be taking her task to heart and was resting up for the event. I let her sleep. I watched her little chest rise and fall, feeling slightly envious. I knew I'd never be able to sleep, though, even for a few moments. Thinking about what Gina was preparing to do wouldn't allow me to slumber.

I was asking a lot of my friend, although in fairness, the portal had been her idea. Still, I knew it wouldn't be an easy spell, and she had other things on her plate that would likely take a lot out of her.

My thoughts were interrupted by the ringing of my cell phone. Even though I caught it on the first ring, it was enough to rouse Daisy, who raised her head and gave me a "you've disturbed me" look.

"Yep?" I said, thinking it would be Nick.

"They're there. They're there now."

It took me a moment to recognize the voice. It was Mark the Dentist. I knew what he meant, but I still asked, "What?" My heart felt suddenly like it had been dipped in ice.

"The Order. They're at Gina's." He sounded like he was crying. Good. "They're going to burn the place down. With her inside."

It was quite a drive to Gina's place, and it was a Saturday night. Traffic would be a bitch. Could I get there in time to make any difference? My mind seemed to be racing but nothing was registering. I tried to collect my wits and blew out a lungful of air. "Now?" was all I could manage to ask.

"I'm supposed to be with them," Mark said miserably. "I… I just can't. I've been thinking. You're right. She doesn't deserve to die. She's not a bad person. She—"

I hung up on the bastard. He'd done what he'd told me he would. He'd alerted me when the Order was ready to act. Unfortunately, from the sounds of it, he hadn't acted quickly enough. They were already at Gina's. He was supposed to give me more time than that.

I speed-dialed Gina's number. There was no answer. I got her voicemail. Fat lot of good that would do. By the time she got the message, the house would be toast, and she might be as well.

I had to move. I grabbed my keys, a jacket, and was out the door in moments. As I raced to my car, I tried to put the jacket on, but my arms kept getting tangled in folds or the wrong holes. Screw it. I threw open the car door and tossed the jacket into the back seat.

I wondered how the Indianapolis Police Department was going to feel about me driving like Steve McQueen through the city streets.

I MADE it to Gina's cottage in a little cul-de-sac in the Irvington area of town in record time. Thankfully, I didn't run over any animals, kids, or old people on the way, although it was a near miss with a raccoon, and I'm sure one older man's heart went into overdrive when he foolishly thought he was safe crossing the street just because the "walk" sign said he could. And the driver of the BMW I nearly collided with may have needed oxygen before continuing his journey. Other than that, the trip was quick, cop free, and devoid of accidents.

Even then, I was too late.

I whipped around the corner onto Gina's street and knew in my bones the Order had already struck. Maybe I could smell the smoke, or maybe it was just a premonition, but I was already slowing the car before I could see the flames licking out of the windows of the Tudor-style home.

The Order had planned it well. The neighbors on either side of Gina's house were obviously out for the night, as their homes were dark. There were no cars parked in Gina's drive, and I assumed her sports car was tucked safely away in her garage, which, so far, was unaffected by the fire. The house, however, was engulfed.

I was out of the car and running up the walk without even thinking. I wasn't sure if I'd even shut off the engine. I wasn't sure I really saw some dark figures darting away from the house or if I imagined them. My mind was on automatic, and little mattered except Gina's safety.

I rushed up to the front door and threw it open, not even bothering to check to see if the knob was hot first. It wasn't, and once I was inside, I saw the flames hadn't yet hit the foyer. I'm not sure I would have cared, though. A burned hand probably wouldn't even have registered.

"Gina!" I called out.

There was no answer save for the roar of the flames.

The side room, where she did her business as a fortune-teller, was a goner. I couldn't even see through the arch leading to the room, the smoke was so thick. Coughing, I tried to fan away some of the smoke to peer within. No go. Everything seemed to be aflame in there.

I could see flames traveling up the walls. In the short hall leading to the back of the house, there was a table that held a few of her framed photographs. It was burning. The wallpaper was crackling and peeling off the walls. I tried to breathe in, but my lungs protested. Coughing and hacking, I knew I had only moments before I would have to get out of the house or become a barbecue myself.

"Gina!" I knew her bedroom was at the back of the house. Avoiding the flames as best I could, I ran toward it. I held a hand up over my mouth in an attempt to keep the smoke out of my lungs.

Outside, I could hear sirens coming closer. Not close enough, though. They wouldn't get there in time to save anyone still in the house.

There were flames licking around the edges of Gina's door, so I knew not to touch the knob. Instead I kicked at the door. It took three kicks, but finally it flew open.

It was even harder to see inside her bedroom than the parlor had been, but soon I could see enough. I could see the bed, awash with flames. I could see the still figure in the bed, a blackened shape that had once been a walking, talking person.

A person who would never walk or talk again.

I WAS sitting at the back of an ambulance, my legs dangling over the edge. The EMT who had earlier insisted on having me suck on an oxygen tank for a few minutes came over and handed me my jacket. I vaguely recalled telling him I'd had one in my car, and he must have retrieved it for me. I thought his name was Jim.

"You might want to put that on," he said gently.

I put it on my lap. The blanket they'd provided for me felt fine around my shoulders, and I didn't want to take the trouble of moving my arms and actually doing something.

"I still think you should go to the hospital and get checked out. Just in case."

I shook my head. I almost said I had little use for hospitals, as I had a friend who was a healing witch who took care of most my injuries, but then I looked again at the husk of a house at the end of the cul-de-sac. The fire had been put out, but firemen were still milling about, checking, I suppose, to make sure some ember wouldn't ignite another blaze. Or maybe they were making sure the body they'd carted out had been the only one. I don't know. I didn't care.

There were people watching the action. Neighborhood people, mostly. Maybe a few who'd been driving by and saw the smoke. The major activity of the night was over, but still they gawked. I wanted to shout at them, ask them if there wasn't something interesting on TV they could watch instead.

Jim—I'm pretty sure that's what his name was—started to walk away, to give me some space. "Thank you," I said.

I think he was surprised to hear my voice. I'd said little since their arrival. I'd told them I'd rushed into the burning house, only to find I'd been too late. I'd told them the owner of the house had been named Gina and she'd been my friend.

Jim paused. He turned and smiled a sad smile at me. "If there's anything I can do," he said.

I shook my head.

I felt like I was in a movie, watching myself on a screen. Everything had a surreal feel to it. The night was definitely cold, but it didn't seem to affect me. The blanket draped over my shoulders was almost more to make the firefighters and EMTs feel better, not me. Like they could somehow ease all my worries with a light wrap. Jim was nice, but I had as much use for nice as I had for the blanket.

I scanned the crowd. There were several people who could have been members of the Order. I hoped they were, that they had come back to check on the aftermath of their deed. If so, I hope they could feel what was in the air. There had been no banishment of evil, just a senseless, pointless act of cruelty.

Another man came over to us and had a whispered conversation with Jim. The guy had a serious countenance and kept nodding as Jim spoke, every now and then making notations on a clipboard he had. Finally, he came over to me.

"Mr. Andrews? I'm Kevin Unger. I need to ask you a few questions."

I was expecting someone would sooner or later grill me over the suspicious nature of the fire. After all, it must have been quite obvious Molotov cocktails or something similar had been used to set the blaze. It was interesting being on the other side of the questioning for once, and I had to say Unger was pretty good at his job. I decided to give him most of what I knew—including seeing shadowy figures running away as I came up to the house. Of course, I left out any mention of the Order of Cotton Mather or that Gina was a witch and her scum boyfriend had been involved, but other than that, I gave it to him straight.

"And you're sure that you couldn't recognize any of the men that you saw running away?" He had asked the same question in various forms several times by the time the interview was winding up.

"They were just dark shapes," I answered. "I saw two or three running toward the back of the house. Strangely enough, it was the fire that concerned me more at that particular moment."

Unger tried a few more questions but finally decided he'd gotten everything out of me I was going to give him. He thanked me and started to walk away.

I stopped him with a question of my own. "Is that it for me, then? Can I go?"

He shook his head sympathetically. "Someone from the police department will want to talk with you, Mr. Andrews. If you could hold on for just a little longer."

It was going to be a long night.

I WAS in a shitty mood, which was a bad thing for the spirit of Dr. Stanley Moore.

Through a series of calls and texts, Nick knew I was going to be delayed, but I hadn't said why. I'm sure he could tell, though, from the lack of details I gave him in response to his questions, that something horrible had happened.

I pulled up at 175 Denmark Street and shut off my engine, feeling angry and tired and a myriad of other emotions, most of which could be summed up by the phrase "pissed off." I sat in my car for a moment, listening to the engine cool.

I closed my eyes, but that wasn't any good. In my mind, I could see the flames shooting up the walls in Gina's house. I could see the framed photograph she had hanging on the wall in her hall. It was a shot of the two of us. She was happy in the picture—heck, we both were. She had her arm around my shoulder and looked like she was pulling me in so she could kiss me. Anyone who didn't know us, looking at that picture, would have thought we were lovers. It hadn't registered when I'd been making my way back to her bedroom, but now I could see that photo bubbling and splitting apart and finally being consumed by the flames.

I couldn't remember who had taken the photo. It couldn't have been Nick, as it had been before we'd met him. Maybe we'd just given the camera to some random stranger and asked them to photograph us. We had been picking pumpkins, that much I recalled.

It killed me to think that I'd never see that picture again.

It was a good thing no members of the Order of Cotton Mather were standing in front of my car at that moment, because I would have restarted the engine and slammed my foot onto the gas before they could move. Then I would have reversed and backed over them, just to make sure.

Robbie, Nick, and Daisy were in Nick's car parked in Jason's driveway, waiting for me. I could see the exhaust coming out of Nick's tailpipe. He must have gotten cold and wanted to run the heater for a while. I was, after all, hours late.

Robbie was in the passenger seat. I could only see Daisy's tail and her big butt, but she was in Nick's arms. Robbie had obviously seen me pull up to the curb, but he hadn't moved to come out to greet me. Maybe there was something in the idea that when you'd been with a person for years, you instinctively knew when to give them space. Nick started to get out, or it looked that way to me, but Robbie must have stopped him. They sat still there waiting for me to exit my car first, the only movement noticeable being Daisy's tail.

I let my eyes travel to the house. I couldn't see much from where I was sitting, just the porch and the lower portion of the building—my car's roof blocked out the rest—but I could feel the energy even from where I was. A black cancer of evil. It's a wonder there weren't For Sale signs up and down the block, families wanting to get away from the sickness that was Moore's old house. My eyes went on, looking at the house next door. It was too dark to read, but there was a yellow sign on the lawn, and it seemed like I could almost make out the Century 21 logo. I snorted out a hollow laugh. Smart people.

Nothing would get done, though, if I continued to sit in the car thinking about burned photographs and things I couldn't change. My left hand seemed to act on its own and reached for the handle. Open door, swing out legs, get to your feet. Yep, that's how you do it. I was surprised to find, as the cold night air hit me, that I was wearing my leather jacket. When had I put that on? It wasn't zipped up, but that was fine. The coolness invigorated me.

Nick shut off his car, and as he opened his door, I heard Daisy bark excitedly. Robbie didn't bother with opening his door; he just sort of glided through it. His face was somber.

"You okay?" he asked.

I nodded. "I'm good."

Ah, how we lie.

Nick was frowning. "Where's Gina? I thought she'd be with you."

Now wasn't the time for explanations. Those could come later, after we'd put the smackdown on our nasty ghostie. "We'll be working without her tonight," I replied, trying not to let any emotion show. "Is everyone ready?"

Daisy certainly was. She was squirming in Nick's arms, eager to get to her task. With the spell Gina had put on her kicking in, she knew the skull she was seeking was nearby, and the dog was chomping at the bit to get to it.

Nick nodded. "Got the charm Gina made for me safely around my neck. Silver dagger strapped to my leg. And the shotguns filled with rock salt are in the trunk." He reached in his pocket and pulled out a small vial. "I've also got this stuff that Gina gave me. When Daisy finds Moore's remains, I'm just supposed to sprinkle this junk on the bones, and poof! At least, that's what she said."

"If that's what she told you," I said, "you can take it that's all you have to do."

Robbie held up his charm, pulling it out from the top of his T-shirt. He seemed really proud of being able to wear something that was new—post-ghost, so to speak. "Got mine on as well. And I can't carry a shotgun or have silver pointy things strapped to me, but...." He thought a moment. "... I do have a sort of cheeky charisma I bring to the group, and a really hot butt." He twisted so he could see a part of his backside. "Seriously, these jeans make it pop, don't you think?"

I knew he was trying to get me to smile, and I was shocked when he succeeded. It wasn't much of a smile, but I appreciated his effort more than his actual words. I loved that little shit more and more every day, and I found solace in the fact that he'd be with me for years and years to come. So I wouldn't have a partner I could have sex with. I'd have one I could love with every fiber of my being, and that was enough.

"Okay," I said. "Let's do this. Nick, you go with Daisy. She'll lead you to the skull. Just try to keep up with her. Meanwhile, Robbie and I will be keeping Moore's ghost busy. We'll give you the time you need to torch his bones, what there is of them."

Nick was forced to set the squirming Daisy onto the ground, and she immediately bounded up to the house, taking the steps leading to the porch so fast it almost seemed her little legs weren't actually making ground contact. I cocked an eyebrow first at Robbie and then at

Nick, as if to say the dog was setting an example for us we had to live up to, if such a complex thought could indeed be transmitted by a mere brow waggle. Whether the intended message was correctly received, I couldn't be sure. However, Nick quickly went to the trunk of his car and removed two shotguns. He tossed one to me.

"Good luck, you guys," he said.

"Same." Inwardly, I added, *Make Gina proud, guys.* After all, her spells and charms would give us our best chance for success in our mission.

When we got up to the front door, Daisy was impatiently waiting for us, making little growling sounds as she shifted her weight back and forth. "Hold on, little girl," I told her as I tried the knob. It was locked. "Not tonight," I said as I took the .38 out of my shoulder holster. Bullets didn't do shit as far as ghosts were concerned, but they worked great on solid objects.

I motioned for Nick to stand back, not wanting him to get hit by flying splinters, and then fired, aiming right at the spot where the bolt would be slid into the frame. The shot seemed unnaturally loud in the quiet night, and I could imagine the reaction of sleeping neighbors. I hoped any who were awakened by the sound would assume it was a car backfiring and simply go back to sleep. One or two might call 911, but the cops would only send a car to check out the street. They wouldn't know to check out Jason Church's house, so we shouldn't have unwary policemen blundering in to worry about.

Besides, I didn't plan on dawdling. In, find the skull, torch it, zap Moore, and out. That was the plan.

Stepping inside, I could feel Moore was waiting for us and that he knew we were armed for battle. The house was even making moans and groans as the wood within shifted with the psychic power Moore was calling on. I could feel the energy rippling through the carpeting under my feet. The walls felt alive as well, sending us negative vibes as if the whole structure was screaming at us. Get out! Run! Before it's too late!

Robbie was right behind me. "Stanley," he called out, "we're home!"

CHAPTER 14

DAISY TOOK a few moments at the threshold, sniffing the air and getting her bearings. Her ears were twitching with excitement. She must have honed in on her objective quickly, though, because she suddenly shot forward, going right through Robbie and between my legs before scampering down the hall.

"After her!" I told Nick.

He switched on his flashlight—the lights, of course, weren't working—and, his shotgun held ready, he took off after the dog. I could see his light bouncing around the walls as he hustled after Daisy until he turned at the end of the hall. In moments, I could hear both him and Daisy heading down the stairs to the basement. I'd suspected that, if Moore's head was indeed in the house, that was where it would be hidden. I just hoped Nick wouldn't encounter any problems in destroying the damned thing once Daisy found it.

"Shall we?" Robbie asked me.

"After you," I said, motioning him to take the lead.

"Oh no, I insist. You first."

"Well, thank you." We were imitating the animated characters Mac and Tosh, the polite gophers in the old Warner Brothers cartoons. Robbie was doing a better job than I was, but I hoped my tone was at least light. If Moore was listening to us, and there was no doubt in my mind he was, we were probably pissing him off, coming across as not worried about him in the least. Good. It wasn't true. I was worried as hell, as there were hundreds of things that could go wrong, especially on Nick's end, but there was no reason to let Moore know of my nervousness.

I switched on my flashlight, cradling the shotgun under my arm. I'd already holstered the .38. As I moved out toward the staircase leading to the second floor, I said to Robbie, "I wish you could hold a flashlight. It would make this a lot easier, and I could have the shotgun ready."

"I could," Robbie said. "For about a minute. Maybe. And then it would slip through my little ghost fingers, and where would we be?"

"In the dark."

"Exactly!"

The sounds around us were increasing in intensity, accompanied now by the phantom wind. I put a foot down on the first step, and the wood creaked so loudly it almost sounded like a human gasp of protest. "He's upstairs," I said.

Behind me, Robbie agreed. "Yeah. And be careful, he's getting ready to hit us with everything he's got. He's even trying to suck my energy out of me again."

"Gina's charm working?"

"So far, so good. I can feel him trying, though."

"If you start to feel weak, get out of here as fast as you can."

Robbie snorted. "Like I'm going to leave you."

"I mean it. I want you safe."

"I'll be fine."

We were moving slowly and carefully, but with each step I took making floorboards emit an alarm, there was little doubt Moore knew exactly where we were. Halfway up the stairs, he started his attack. A candlestick that had been on a table in the foyer suddenly flew across the room, hitting the opposite wall with a thud. Ahead of us, a framed picture rattled violently against the wall before the wire holding it in place snapped, and it crashed to the ground, hitting the top step and tumbling down until it hit my leg. I kicked it aside.

"It seems," I said, turning to Robbie, "that the doctor is in."

"Maybe we should have called ahead for an appointment."

An ashtray sailed from somewhere in the front room and shot up the stairs with enough force and speed that I had no time to react. The damned thing hit me in the left shoulder, and I cried out as the pain shot through me. Instinctively, I dropped the flashlight in order to grab my injured shoulder. The flashlight bounced down a couple of steps before stopping, its light extinguished. It was hard to tell with the wind and moans, but I thought I detected the sound of the glass shield breaking. It hardly mattered.

"I like the dark, anyway," I said through clenched teeth as I rubbed my shoulder. At least I still had the shotgun under my now-damaged left arm.

Robbie reached out, wanting to put a comforting hand on my shoulder, but of course I felt nothing. Suddenly, he looked up. The upstairs was in near total darkness, but I could just about make out the frame of the door to the middle bedroom. As I watched, a light suddenly shone around the edges of the door, growing in intensity.

"The doctor will see us now," Robbie quipped.

The wind was cold, but I ignored the goose bumps. My concentration was all on the door before us and the ever-brightening light behind it, but I noticed, out of the corner of my eye, that Robbie's hair was being whipped about by the gusts. Phantom hair, phantom winds. I wondered, briefly, if he was feeling the chill.

I didn't have the chance to ask. With an enormous crash, the door flew open, and standing there in the frame was the tall, black figure of Dr. Stanley Moore. He glared at me and then at Robbie. He didn't look worried.

He opened his mouth to speak, but before the words even left his mouth, I fired one barrel of the shotgun right at his chest. The light coming from the room was almost blinding, but all I had to do was shoot at the dim figure in the doorway, and at that distance, I couldn't miss.

Moore vanished as the pellets hit him. I turned to Robbie. "I couldn't care less what the bastard had to say."

"He's still here," Robbie warned.

He was right. The rock salt may have dissipated the spirit, but the wind and the roaring in our ears continued. Normally, a good blast of salt would make a ghost go away for quite some time while it slunk off to lick its wounds and regain strength. If that had been the case with Moore, however, his ghostly manifestations—the wind, the moaning—would have stopped as well.

"Shit," I said, just as the doctor reappeared right next to me. He made a small gesture with his hand, and the shotgun flew out of my hands, flying across the hall. Not that it mattered much, seeing as how much effect the one barrel had on our friend. Another blast would have only gained us a second or two.

Still, I could have used those seconds. When you were fighting a megapowerful spirit, the one thing you didn't want to be was right next to him, in reach of his grubby little hands. And Moore's right hand reached out with preternatural speed and grasped me by the throat.

His fingers felt more than solid as they squeezed into my flesh. It was as if my neck had suddenly been put into a vise. I beat against the arm stopping me from getting fresh oxygen into my lungs, to no avail. It was like hitting a statue. He tightened the grip of his fingers. I kicked out, but that didn't seem to bother Moore in the slightest.

My chest began to ache, and my vision started to darken. Time seemed to slow down, and I could hear Robbie shouting something. He sounded very far away, which I knew he wasn't, and distorted, like he was underwater.

I knew if I didn't get some air into my lungs soon, I was a goner. I managed to get my hands up to my throat and attempted to pry Moore's fingers away. I could feel other fingers trying to do the same, so Robbie was trying to help. I couldn't see him, though. I couldn't see much of anything. Even the light coming from the bedroom seemed to be fading.

Come on, Nick, my brain screamed. *We need that skull torched now!*

It seemed like the only thing I could see were Moore's eyes. I could see evil in them, but something else as well. Maybe it was my psychic sense, or maybe Moore was allowing me to see the scene so he could gloat in my dying seconds, but I saw Nick and Daisy.

They were in the basement, in an old coal room. Daisy had found a spot in the wall with a hidden cache, and Nick, finally understanding why the dog was staring at the wall and barking, began to feel around the bricks until he found one that shifted. He pressed against it, and a hidden door slid open. The section of the wall where the coal chute had once been was covered with wood, and a little door was revealed about a foot from the floor. Nick got down and quickly swung the door all the way open, and I saw him cringe as he saw what was hidden inside.

Moore's skull was in a cavity in the wall, brown with age and decay. A cockroach crawled out of the eye socket and scampered down the cheekbone. Daisy gave a triumphant bark as Nick scrambled to get the vial Gina had given him out of his pocket.

Before he could do so, though, the room filled with ghosts. Moore's victims. His army.

I could see the sorrow in their eyes. They didn't want to interfere with Nick and what he was doing, but they had no choice. Seven young men, their lives cut short in their prime. All had died horribly, and some of them showed their wounds in death. One young man who didn't look like he could have been over seventeen had a hole in his chest. Moore had cut out his heart. Another had had his throat slit from ear to ear and phantom blood still gushed from the wound. One, a farm-boy type, a good-looking, strapping lad, was naked. His genitals had been cut off. Although, from the ragged look of the wound, they might have been bitten off.

Nick glanced quickly around. He had, it seemed, left his shotgun over by the door. The ghosts were between him and the gun. Nick stood. I saw his mouth moving, but I couldn't hear what he was saying. He must have been trying to explain to the sad ghosts that he was trying to help them, that he was going to set them free.

If they understood, they were unable to stop themselves. They slowly ambled forward, reaching out for Nick. He stood, one hand out in a placating gesture and the other still trying in vain to retrieve the vial. The ghost with no genitals was closest, and it reached out to grab Nick, who backpedaled several paces. Unfortunately, he tripped over Daisy, who had rushed forward, barking madly—although I couldn't hear her, her mouth was going like crazy. Nick went down hard and hit his head against the brick wall as he fell. He was obviously unconscious as he struck the floor, and I could see a trickle of blood coming from his temple where he'd collided with the wall.

Moore blinked and the vision went away. All I could see was his hateful face smiling at me as he choked the life from me. "There's no help coming for you," he said. I wasn't sure the words were said aloud or if they were just projected into my head. Not that it mattered. I could feel myself passing out.

Well, at least Robbie and I would be in the same boat now.

I made a last attempt to get the strong fingers off my throat, but I could feel the strength leaving my body. It was futile. The bastard was just too strong. My legs seemed to give out, and if Moore's hands hadn't been holding me up I would have fallen to the floor. He had pressed me back until I was against the balcony rail that ran from the top of the stairs and across the part of the hall that overlooked the foyer. Maybe I could shove myself back and throw myself over. I'd still die, probably, but at least I'd be robbing Moore of the pleasure of being the one who snuffed me.

Suddenly, the front door flew open. I heard it more than saw it, as my vision was almost nil, but I could tell the movement surprised Moore even more than me. He even loosened his grip slightly, and I gasped, getting a tiny bit of wonderful, wonderful air into my lungs. His fingers were still clamped tightly around my throat, but the distraction gave me, literally, breathing space. My vision even returned from the blackness. A bit.

Moore had been sneering into my face, but now he frowned as he looked down into the foyer. A young woman entered. She was smallish, thin, and had long black hair the wind was throwing into a frenzy. Her pace was slow, confident. And her eyes burned with power.

"Hello, boys," she said in a voice I didn't recognize. "Did you miss me?"

Moore growled and almost thrust me aside. Unfortunately, he didn't release me. I slumped down, my knees almost hitting the floor.

Robbie scrambled to my side, looking as solid as I'd ever seen him. He pried at the fingers holding me up.

"Hold on, Duncan," he said, panic in his voice. "I've got ya."

Moore made a gesture with his free hand, and the hall mirror jerked away from the wall and went flying. It sailed over the balustrade and would have hit the woman with dark hair, but she made a tiny movement of her hand, and before the mirror reached her, it crashed to the floor as if it had hit an invisible barrier. Which, I suppose, it had.

The woman smiled. "Oh no, you don't."

For the first time, I saw something new in Moore's eyes. Worry.

All of a sudden, he released his grip on me. I sank down the rest of the way to the floor, clutching at my throat, trying to get it working properly again. Air, beautiful air. I'd never take it for granted again.

Robbie was at my side, and he was holding me in his arms. It took me a moment to realize I could actually feel his arms around me. I guess his ghost adrenaline was kicking in, giving him extra power. More oomph. Whatever the cause, I liked the feeling. He looked at me, and I saw love and worry and more in his eyes. He seemed to reluctantly glance at the woman down in the foyer, a frown on his face.

"I think," he said, "that the cavalry has arrived. I don't know who she is, but she's pissed!"

I turned my head slightly and looked through the banisters. Down below us, the dark-haired woman strode forward. She raised her hands into the air and shouted above the roar of the wind. "Spirits of the air and earth, I call to thee! I wish to open a portal, a portal that cannot be but is. A portal that will take this evil, accursed soul to where he needs to be. Where he deserves to be!"

The air behind Moore seemed to shimmer and coalesce. The woman waved her arms again and a bright light appeared out of nowhere, a beam about six feet high and two feet across, a mere foot from where Moore stood. The light was nearly blinding, so much so that Robbie and I, and even Moore, had to shield our eyes from it. The only person unaffected seemed to be the woman.

She had reached the bottom of the staircase. "Step back, Stanley Moore. Step back into the void. You cannot resist the pull. You must go into the light and be delivered to where you are meant to go." The woman paused on the bottom step, a thin smile playing about her lips. "In short, go to hell."

The air behind Moore convulsed, and he seemed to be pulled back. He was nearly within the vortex, but he was fighting it with all his might.

"You must go in!" the woman shouted. "You have no choice!"

Moore growled in anguish as he seemed to be sucked backward. He gritted his teeth, and with obvious effort, he yanked himself forward. He only got a few inches, but it seemed to be enough that he was no longer in danger of being pulled into the portal. A grin crossed his face, and he reached down and grabbed me by my jacket collar. With a roar, he yanked me away from Robbie and nearly to my feet.

"Robbie!" the woman yelled. "Duncan mustn't touch the portal!"

Moore was trying to force me to step into the unearthly light, but I had regained enough strength to put up a fight. I knew Moore was powerful, so I concentrated on getting away from him, which didn't really require much. I bent forward. He had my collar solidly in his grip, but if I could move just right, shrugging my arms out of the coat, I'd be free.

I managed it, just. My left arm caught on the sleeve as I was wiggling free, but it was enough to get away from the bastard. I hit the balustrade hard, and for the briefest of seconds, I thought I would go over, but I regained my balance just in time.

"Damn you!" Moore roared as he tossed my jacket aside. The portal still raged behind him, but he was no longer close enough to it for it to be a danger for him. If I could shove myself forward and push him….

Moore growled again, holding out his hands. He seemed to be sucking in as much energy as he could. Robbie had risen to his feet and backed away a few paces. I could tell from the look on his face that part of the energy Moore was accumulating was coming from him, and Robbie was fighting it with all his might.

The dark-haired woman was halfway up the stairs when Moore shot out his hand. I felt energy flowing out of him like a concentrated hurricane, and it burst forward and hit the woman right in the chest. She flew back, landing at the bottom of the stairs without even hitting a step. She grunted in pain as she hit the floor and rolled over. She stirred and groaned but was obviously very hurt.

Moore strode forward, grinning. He grabbed me again, by the face this time. I could feel his strong fingers digging into my flesh. One finger was on my cheek, and I wondered how much pressure he could exert before the bone broke. Another of his digits was right on my eyeball, pressing in.

I leaned back, trying to loosen his grip. I was halfway over the banister, one hand holding on to the rail for dear life and the other attempting to get Moore off me. I managed to twist my face away from him, and while he still had a hold on me, at least now my eyeball wasn't in danger of being punctured.

I could see Robbie out of the corner of my eye, scared and not knowing what to do. He glanced at the woman, who was stirring but still fairly out of it. He returned his gaze to me, and I knew he saw that in seconds, I would be flipped over the banister, probably to break my neck. Robbie bit his lip and a look of sadness filled his eyes.

"I love you, Duncan," he said, the words barely audible over the howl of the phantom wind.

And then he turned his attention to Moore, and his face twisted in anger. "You motherfucker!" he shouted as he barreled forward.

Robbie hit Moore right in the midsection with a football tackle, sending them both backward. Moore screamed as the portal swallowed the two of them up, and the light convulsed as they disappeared within the beam. And then it was gone.

The light was gone. Moore was gone. But so was Robbie.

"No!" I yelled as I sank to the floor, my legs not wanting to hold up my weight. I couldn't be seeing right. Or Robbie would come right back. He'd be lying there on the floor, and we'd go home and be happy, and everything would be right with the world.

I crawled over to the spot where the portal had formed, hoping to feel some residual energy there, something that would give me hope that what I'd seen hadn't been real. Robbie couldn't be gone. My fingers ran over the carpet. There was nothing. "No," I repeated, panic rising within me.

I put my hand into the air, hoping the portal would reappear. Nothing. It was gone, and so was my love.

"No."

The house felt different. Moore was gone, along with all his manifestations. No phantom wind. No moans from the house. I could tell even the ghosts of his victims were gone, released from his hold. They were now at peace. The house was just a house now. Not that it mattered. Nothing mattered, at least not to me. Robbie was gone.

Distantly, I heard voices. Nick. He must have recovered and come back up from the basement. I could even hear the little patter made by Daisy's feet as she walked along the hardwood floor downstairs.

"Is it over?" Nick asked. He must have seen the woman, because he asked, "Um… who are you?"

Time didn't seem to make sense to me. I felt hands on my shoulders. I think the touch was meant to be comforting, but I was unable to be comforted. "Duncan?" the woman asked. She was kneeling next to me. So was Nick. There was a trickle of blood running down his face. Daisy was there as well. But no Robbie.

"He's… I can't…." I tried to say something, but the words weren't making sense. Not surprising. My head wasn't functioning. I felt numb.

Their hands tried to gently pull me to my feet. I let them. Someone—it must have been Nick—was on my other side, lifting me by my elbow. "It's over, Duncan. The house is cleared. Moore's spirit is gone."

That was supposed to make me feel better? "Robbie," I said. It was supposed to be a question, as in "What about Robbie?" but it came out flat, just his name.

"He's gone," the woman said sadly. "But the portal would have taken him to a good place. It takes people to where they're supposed to be. I'm sure he's happy, if that's any consolation."

It wasn't.

CHAPTER 15

I DIDN'T sleep that night. What would have been the point? At first light, I got into my car to drive to Greenwood Cemetery, a place I hadn't been in years. Hell, there hadn't been a reason to go there before. Now, though, I felt compelled to visit. Robbie's grave was there, and I hoped I'd find some answers, maybe some sense that, if he was truly gone, at least he was happy. I needed to know.

Before the cemetery, I stopped off at the Hilton downtown. I didn't have to get out of the car or even put money in the meter. The woman with the long black hair was waiting for me by the entrance, wearing a white coat. It had started to snow. When she got into my passenger seat, I noticed a few flakes adhering to her shoulders and the back of her coat and in her hair.

She smiled gently. "How are you doing, Duncan?"

"Rotten," I said as I pulled away from the curb.

She reached over and put her hand on my leg. "You know, I'm so sorry. But he did it to save you."

I didn't say anything. That's the good thing with friends: you don't always have to talk. We drove in silence for several minutes. Finally, I glanced over at her. "I wasn't expecting shorter."

She shrugged. "Neither was I. With transmogrification, you never know exactly what you're going to get."

"And the black hair. Nice touch."

She ran a hand through it. "It's a bit long for my liking, but I'm sure I'll get used to it."

"Do I still call you Gina?"

She thought about that. "Well, to the rest of the world, I'll have to have a different name, or otherwise this all will be for nothing, and the Order of Cotton Mather will just try again. But I think it's okay for you to call me Gina." She frowned. "Maybe I should go by my full name. Regina. What do you think?"

I shook my head. "Gina."

She patted my leg. "Gina it is."

"I'm sure you've got tons of questions—" she started to say.

"Not really," I answered

That got a smile out of her. "Well, I have a few of my own. Namely about the body you supplied that was supposed to be me."

"I got it from a friend of mine. A demon I call Elton."

"I understand that, but what I can't figure out is…." She paused. "The body looked like me. Hell, when I put her in the bed, it seemed like I was arranging my doppelgänger. Duncan, she *was* me."

"Had to be convincing. This way, even the dental records will match."

"I don't have dental records. I've never been to a dentist. No need."

I hadn't thought of that. "Well, everything will match, in any case. There won't be any question that my friend, Gina, died in that fire."

Gina took a deep breath before saying, "Demons don't have that sort of power. Your friend, Elton, couldn't have done that, made a body look like me. What gives, Duncan?"

I couldn't tell her about my meeting, vision quest, whatever it was, with her father, Eleazar. Or could I? No, better not. Eleazar hadn't wanted it known that he'd helped out, so I'd best keep it just between him and me. So I shrugged. "Maybe Elton picked up a few tricks over the years."

I could tell she was unconvinced, but she didn't press the point. Instead, she sighed. "I wish I didn't have to lose my house and all my stuff. I'll miss that stuff."

"So will I," I said.

She smiled. "Oh, I saved a lot of the best things. The really good charms and potions. But the personal stuff is what I'll miss most. My pictures, my furniture. My clothes." She looked down at her now smaller body. "Not that anything would fit any longer. But the shoes. Damn it, I really miss the shoes."

"We'll buy out a shoe store, set you up all over again."

"And I'll need a new job. Something different, since I'm supposed to be someone new."

"Maybe you could work in a shoe shop. Kill two birds with one stone." We were getting close to the cemetery. Traffic was thin, but I found myself slowing down the closer we got. Was I afraid to see Robbie's grave, now that I was so close? Would seeing it make me believe he was really gone for good?

I felt empty. Like part of me had been cut away. A part I loved.

I pulled into the cemetery and went past the gates. I knew vaguely where Robbie's grave was, even though it had been over ten years since I'd been there. A sign warned me not to go over ten miles an hour. No problem. I was in no hurry.

"I'll have one of my contacts get some ID papers for you. Driver's license. Social Security Card. That sort of thing."

"I take it this will be one of your less reputable contacts?"

"Well, reputable contacts don't know how to print up that kind of shit."

We were there, but I didn't want to get out of the car. I parked but didn't shut off the engine.

"We don't have to do this, Duncan," Gina said.

I closed my eyes. "I have to."

"He loved you very much."

I closed my eyes tighter. I knew my cheeks were flushing with anger. Anger at myself for living. Anger at Robbie for throwing his existence away to save me. "I know, but... he shouldn't...." I couldn't say more.

"He did it to save you. It was his choice. You have to respect that."

The anger faded and despair took its place. I opened the car door. "Let's do this," I said.

It took several minutes to find his grave. I had remembered it being closer to the oak tree that oversaw that section of the cemetery, but in actuality, it wasn't all that close. Finally, I located the plaque in the ground. Robert Randall Church, followed by the dates of his birth and his death. There should be another date, the one he'd actually left me on.

I touched the marker. I didn't know what I expected. Maybe something that would tell me Robbie was in heaven and happy and waiting for me. But I just felt cold stone.

Gina seemed to read my mind, for she said, "The portal would have sent him to where he belonged. He'll be in heaven, Duncan."

And what, I wanted to ask, was I supposed to do in the meantime, while I was still alive? I couldn't contemplate going on without him. Aloud, I said, "It's funny. When Robbie announced that he wanted to move on and even set a date for New Year's, I knew I'd be crushed when he went, but I thought I could handle it. After all, our relationship was a mess. I was alive. He wasn't. It was goddamned impossible. But this." I shook my head. "It wasn't supposed to happen like this. This is just wrong."

"Sometimes things happen," Gina said. "People come into our lives. They leave them. Sometimes abruptly. It sucks, but that's life. I guess you just have to cherish the time you had with them."

And I'd had an extra ten years plus with Robbie few others could have had. I should have been happy about that, but it was hard to feel anything other than emptiness. I ran my fingers over the letters of his name, hoping it would make me feel connected to him.

"I called Nick earlier," Gina said, probably to get my mind on other things. "To see if he was okay. He got a nasty crack on the head last night."

I was glad Nick was okay. "I'll check in on him later."

Now that I was at the gravesite, I was reluctant to leave. Gina stood back, the snowflakes catching in her black hair and on her new face. It was going to take a while for me to get used to the fact that she now had a totally different body.

"I'll give you a few minutes by yourself, if you like," she said softly.

"I'd like that."

She moved away. I turned back to the marker and ran my fingers over his name again. My fingers were cold, but I was glad I hadn't brought gloves. I needed the tactile feel of the stone. I sighed deeply.

"I should have a ton to say." I forced a slight smile. If he could hear me—and if there was any sense to the universe, he could—he'd expect a smile from me. "It's odd, but with all the talk of you leaving and us moving on and all that crap, you'd think I'd have been prepared for this. But I wasn't. I guess a person never can be.

"I could go on, but you know me. You know how I feel. You'll always be with me. And I'll love you always."

A snowflake caught in my eyelashes. I blinked and realized I was crying. It hit me so fast that the tears had started without me even knowing. "I...." I couldn't talk. My voice just cracked.

When Gina came back over to me, I was sobbing so hard my shoulders were shaking.

TWO DAYS later, the day after Thanksgiving, I opened the door at 175 Denmark Street and stood aside, ushering Jason, Anthony, and Gary to enter first. They hesitated, not surprisingly. "It's perfectly safe," I said. "Promise."

They looked hopeful, but still no one moved. I hoped one of them would take the plunge, because it was bitterly cold out, and even though I was wearing my heaviest coat, I was shivering. My cheeks felt numb, and my fingers seemed undecided as to whether they should just snap off or not. I really had to buy some gloves. Nick was standing behind the trio, and he was hunching his shoulders in an attempt to bury his head within the coat he was wearing.

Finally, Gary pushed past his dads and walked across the threshold. "It's gotta be warmer inside, if nothing else," he said.

Anthony and Jason quickly followed. Nick was right on their heels. I entered last, shutting the door behind me.

I'd come by earlier to make sure the thermostat was set at a decent temperature, so the house was toasty warm. I didn't want any cold spots causing the householders to wonder, even in the back of their minds, if the house might still be haunted.

I didn't know if Jason noticed the warmth, but he was wandering around the front room, gazing up at the second floor. His face, at first showing skepticism, was now full of amazement. "It... it has a totally different feel in here now. It's.... I don't know."

Anthony nodded. "Even the air feels lighter."

"It's a home now," I said. "The place is yours again. I hope you guys decide to stay. This place could use a little love."

Gary bounded up the stairs. He glanced around the upstairs hall and then looked down over the balustrade at us. "The mirror's gone!"

"Yeah." I smiled. "I figured a few things might carry bad memories, so I took them away. I can return it, if you like."

Jason turned to me. "I'd be perfectly happy if I never saw that damned thing again."

Gary started to open the door to the middle bedroom upstairs, but a warning from Anthony stopped him. "Hold on," his father said. "I'm not sure you—"

"The house is clear," I assured him. "Entirely. There's nothing to worry about."

Nick and I stood in the foyer while the others went from room to room, getting more and more excited as the truth of my words began to sink in. Nick's hands were jammed into his front pockets. "It's hard to believe," he said, "that this is even the same house. It seems brighter."

"It is," I agreed. "Haunted houses—especially megahaunted ones—tend to suck in even energy from sunlight. So even on the sunniest of days, they're just a tad darker than they should be."

"It doesn't even seem like the same place." Nick took in a deep breath, and I could tell he was reaching out with his senses. "The ghosts of his victims are gone as well. There's nothing here."

"Once they weren't under Moore's control, they were able to move on. I'm sure they're in a better place."

Nick put a hand on my shoulder. "You doing okay?"

I thought about that a moment. "Yes. And no. In one way, I feel like I'll never be totally okay again. I feel like a huge chunk has been taken out of my life, and there's only this gaping hole left. But on the same hand, I feel that he's gone on to a better place. I know that. I keep telling myself that's the important thing, and how I feel should be secondary."

With an encouraging smile, Nick rubbed his hand across my back. "He's happy. I know that."

There had been a time when Nick touching me would have brought conflicting feelings, but now I just felt friendship. And God knew I needed friends. I sighed. "I went to his grave the other day. I thought that I'd get some sense of him there so I'd know for sure that he was happy. I felt nothing."

Nick removed his hand. Jason and the guys were in the basement, and we could hear Gary give out a triumphant whoop. Nick laughed. "I think they're finally convinced that Moore's ghost is really gone."

"They've been through a lot. But I hope they decide to stay here."

A look of worry crossed Nick's face. "The skull...."

"Torched. Did it yesterday. Moore was gone for good, but I thought it should be put to dust anyway, just in case. Besides, it made me feel good doing it."

Hesitatingly, Nick asked, "Did you tell Jason about...."

"Robbie?" I nodded. "When I called him to tell him we'd succeeded. I thought he should know how brave his cousin is." I paused. "Was."

We both instinctively looked upstairs to the spot where Robbie had shoved Moore into the portal. "I wish I'd recovered quicker," Nick said. "Maybe I could have—"

I shook my head. "Believe me, I've gone all over the could-have-beens and should-have-beens. I should have moved away from the railing when I had the chance. I should have shoved Moore back myself, somehow getting the bastard in without touching it myself. But could-have-beens don't change what happened."

I tore my eyes away as they began to water. Suddenly, I wanted out of the house. Hell, I wanted out of Indianapolis. Maybe I should take a vacation. A long one. Nothing was stopping me now. I wasn't restricted to only going to places Robbie had been when he'd been alive. I could hit a beach down in Florida or travel to England. A castle tour. That sounded good.

Except what was the good of seeing some old castle when you couldn't share the experience with the one you loved?

A tear found its way down my cheek, and I turned so Nick couldn't see it. Not that I was embarrassed. More that I didn't want to burden him with my feelings. And maybe a little embarrassment. We macho types with big hearts had to walk a fine line. Show too little emotion, and you're a cold brick. Too much, and you might as well start quoting Dr. Oz and watching Hallmark movies while eating bonbons.

"What are you thinking?"

I closed my eyes. "I'm thinking I don't know how I'm going to make it without him."

Sometimes you just had to say to hell with macho and let the inner Hallmark out.

"SO WHAT size do you wear now?" I asked.

Gina—she had put the kibosh on me calling her Gina 2.0—arched an eyebrow. "I notice you ask me now, after I've already bought out Macy's for a new wardrobe." She sighed. "I'll miss the black, flowing things, though. Still, if I'm going to be a new person, I might as well dress new as well."

"Christmas is coming up. I might want to add to your wardrobe."

"Forget clothes. Find me a place to live."

We were enjoying an afternoon cup of tea at my place. A week had gone by since Robbie had gone, and I still didn't like to spend much time there by myself, even with Daisy to keep me company. The place was too quiet, too empty. Gina seemed to realize this, and we'd been spending evenings together, watching television and playing cards. I'd had two cases offered to me. One was a missing persons case, and one was an older lady who was convinced her brother was possessed by Theodore Roosevelt. I declined them both, mainly because I didn't feel like going back to work yet, but also because the missing persons case was too pedestrian, and the other was likely due to the woman having watched *Arsenic and Old Lace* on the late movie. If her brother began to brandish a sword and take to running up the stairs yelling, "Charge!" I might change my mind and look into it, but I thought that unlikely.

I looked at the woman sitting across the kitchen table from me. She was just setting down her cup. She licked a drop of tea from her lips. "You're welcome to stay here," I said. "Plenty of room."

"No, there isn't," she replied. "Besides, I have no ambition to start up a paranormal *Will & Grace*." She wiggled her eyebrows and reached into her black bag, the same one she'd always kept her most important potions and charms and whatnot in. She'd made sure it hadn't been in the house when it burned. "Speaking of my new life, I now officially have a new identity. Your friend supplied me with papers." She pulled out a manila envelope. "I've got a passport, a Social Security Card, and a birth certificate. He did a good job, I must say. Although I'm not sure about the name."

"What is it?"

"Georgiana Lynn Walters. I sound like the heroine of a Harlequin romance novel."

"Well, Georgiana," I said, ignoring the glare the name got me, "have you given any thought to work? It wouldn't be advisable to set up another fortune-telling business."

Gina smiled. "Oh, I've got that covered as well." She pulled a thick paper out of the envelope and showed it to me. "It seems I graduated from Indiana University. I'm thinking about becoming a teacher."

"Really? I wouldn't have thought that was something you'd be interested in."

"Nonsense! I love kids. Besides, every kid thinks his or her teacher is a witch. This time, they'll be right."

I slid the envelope closer to me and fished inside. "Let's see this driver's license."

"It's a horrible picture."

Examining the document in question, I said, "According to this, you're only twenty-four years old."

"Well, I look about that age now."

"No, you don't."

Gina tried to look stern, but with limited success. "You could be turned into a newt, you know."

"I've had worse things happen to me." The words were spoken lightly, but they still brought a sad gleam into Gina's eyes. With an overly chipper voice, I said, "Well, enough of this. Shall we break out the cards? Or do you want me to whoop you in Monopoly again?"

She shook her head and rose from the table. "Not tonight. I'm going apartment hunting. Come with me."

It was tempting, but I shook my head. At some point I was going to have to get used to an evening in the apartment sans Robbie. "I'm good," I said.

"Are you sure? I'm going to be up in the Castleton area. We can hit the mall afterward and then get some dinner."

I got up as well and fetched her coat from the stand by the door. "I'm sure," I said, helping her into it. I watched her arms as she positioned them for the sleeves. "My God, your arms are skinny now."

"I had to do the spell quickly. There wasn't time for tweaking. Be glad I didn't come out looking like a combination of Bella Abzug and Joan Rivers."

"Is it like *Doctor Who*?" I asked. "You know, you regenerate, and you've got a new body and a slightly different personality?"

She glared at me. "Remember. Newt. I can do it."

I shook my head. "Nope, same old personality."

She really couldn't turn people into newts, but it was a standing joke between us. At least, I didn't think she could.

Daisy had come to the door to help see Gina out. Gina leaned down to pat her head. "Keep an eye on him. If he starts to get maudlin, you call me," she said to the dog.

I could have sworn Daisy nodded her head.

Two minutes after shutting the door behind Gina, I began to think I should have gone with her. I sat on the couch and picked up the remote, but the only thing I could find even slightly interesting on TV was an episode of *Supernatural*, and I realized, after watching a scene or two, that it was a repeat. I switched off the set and got up to find a book I hadn't read. I was scanning my bookshelves when I heard a very light knocking at the door. It was, in fact, so light, that if it hadn't brought forth a series of barks from Daisy, I would have concluded I imagined it.

"Just a minute," I said, thinking it must be Gina having forgotten something. Before I got to the door, the knocking sounded again. As before, it was so faint that whoever it was must have been barely brushing their knuckles against the door.

I paused before turning the knob and felt with my senses. There was no paranormal warning, so the caller was human. Maybe it was one of the neighbor kids, wanting to get a look at the weird bulldog. I opened the door.

I blinked, because what I saw was impossible. But the vision didn't disappear.

Robbie was standing there, a slight grin on his face. He was nude and looked exhausted. He swayed slightly as he said, "Eleazar and his buddies say hi."

And then he collapsed into my arms.

CHAPTER 16

ROBBIE WAS in bed—in our bed—unconscious. His chest was rising and falling, so he was breathing. As a ghost, he'd "breathe" or at least simulate the action, whether from habit or a weird ghostly trace memory, I never really knew. But now his nostrils flared slightly with each intake of oxygen. He was actually breathing. It was shallow, but it was there.

Gina was leaning over him. She'd already opened up his eyelids, felt his chest, and was now gripping his wrist to feel for a pulse. She waited a moment and then slid his arm under the covers and pulled them up to his chin. He stirred and licked his lips but didn't wake.

"He's alive," Gina said, her voice a mix of skepticism and confidence. "I don't know how, but he's alive. Human. Definitely human."

Nick was standing a few feet away from the foot of the bed, as if he expected Robbie to spontaneously combust or sprout wings at any moment. "It's like he never died. Still looks the same." He turned to me. "You say he just appeared at your door?"

"Naked as a jaybird," I answered. When I'd called Gina and Nick, I'd told them to come over immediately. I hadn't said why. Well, it was something they'd have to see to believe, anyway. If I'd said, "Come quick. Robbie's alive," they'd have notified the guys in the white coats and had them on standby. Hell, I still didn't believe my eyes.

"It's impossible," Gina asserted. She placed a hand over Robbie's forehead. "No fever." She closed her eyes, and I could tell she was reading his mind. "It's Robbie. Not some doppelgänger or shape-shifter or anything like that. It's him." She opened her eyes. "But it's impossible!

No one has the power to do that, especially after over a decade of being dead. It would take the combined power of the Council of Witches to…." She eyed me questioningly. "But they'd never do that. It's unheard of. Unprecedented. Even my father wouldn't…. Duncan, what aren't you telling me?"

I shook my head. "I don't know how he's here. When I opened the door, he was standing there, and all he said was that Eleazar and the boys said hi."

"But they wouldn't… they couldn't…." Gina's new face was set in a deep frown.

"I think they did." I sat on the edge of the bed and ran my hand across Robbie's cheek. Skin. Warm, living skin. He sighed in his sleep. "Maybe your dad convinced the Council to do me a favor in return for helping save you from the Order of Cotton Mather."

"I suppose that's possible, but if you ever met the Council—and I've only seen them in visions—they're a hard group to convince to do anything." She stared at Robbie's face. "My God, he's got long eyelashes. It was hard to see them properly when he was a ghost. I'd kill to have lashes like that. Now I've got skimpy lashes. I lost my old ones along with my blonde hair and taller body."

I bent over and kissed Robbie's forehead. Again, the moist, warm skin almost came as a shock to me. I wasn't used to it. "Why hasn't he woken up? Is he okay?"

"He's fine," Gina assured me. "He's just tired. Worn out. Whatever happened to bring him back, it took a lot out of him." She shook her head. "The only way they could have done this… they must have pulled him out of time, taken him right before his car accident, and transported him here, now."

"You mean," I asked, "that when he wakes up, he's going to wonder why I look so much older, and wonder why Daisy looks the way she does, and he won't know who the two of you are, and—"

"Duncan, you're babbling!" Gina smiled gently. She indicated that she wanted to sit where I was. "May I?"

I got up and watched as she settled next to Robbie's sleeping form and once again put a hand on his forehead. Closing her eyes, she said, "I'm going to see if I can search his memory." She frowned in concentration. "No, he's fine. If I'm correct, and they pulled him out of time, and I think I must be, otherwise there would be no body to put him into, they must also have restored his memory of the last ten years." She opened her eyes. "He'll remember being a ghost."

"Holy shit," Nick muttered. He shook his head in confusion. "Wait. I mean, he still looks like he's twenty. But he's had about thirty years of memories. Is he twenty or thirty?" He put a hand up to his temple. "That makes my head hurt just thinking about it."

"Yours?" I asked. "My head hasn't stopped spinning since he knocked on the door."

Gina glared at us. "We're presented with a miracle, and the two of you are concerned with how many candles to put on his next birthday cake? Get some perspective, will you!"

From her spot by the doorway, Daisy yapped as if to signal her agreement with Gina.

As soon as Gina rose, I took her place by Robbie's side, running my hand through his hair. "I can't stop touching him. I can't get over that I *can* touch him."

Gina was pacing alongside the bed, puzzling it all out. "Duncan, have you been in contact with my father?"

My eyes stayed on Robbie's lovely face when I answered her. "If I had, he probably told me that I shouldn't tell you or anyone else about it."

She made a sour face. "That sounds like my dad. So secretive. I wonder who he thought I'd tell?" She paced some more. "That body you got from your demon friend—"

"Elton."

"—looked just like me. I mean, it was a doppelgänger. A dead me." She glanced down at her body. "Well, the old me. A demon couldn't have done that, but my father could transmogrify a dead body in his sleep."

"If that's your idea of a good time," Nick said.

Gina ignored the interruption. "So you and Dad come up with a plan to ensure the Order is convinced I'm dead. In return, he coerces the Council to restore Robbie to life."

I shrugged. "It wasn't part of the deal." I realized I was making an admission, so I added, "If, indeed, there was any sort of communication between your father and me." I didn't want to piss off the old guy, especially now. What if he changed his mind because I blabbed too much? "Anyway, let's not worry about it. He's here, it's a miracle, blah, blah." In my best Michael Palin voice from *Monty Python and the Holy Grail*, I added, "Let's not argue about who resurrected whom."

"Who's that supposed to be?" Gina asked. I told her and she said, "That's the worst impression I've ever heard."

I shook my head. "Everyone's a critic."

Robbie groaned softly and moved his head from side to side.

"I think he's waking up," Gina said. She grasped Nick by the elbow. "Come on. Let's leave them alone for now."

They had been out of the room for nearly five minutes before Robbie opened up his eyes. When he saw me leaning over him, grinning like an idiot, a smile crossed his face as well. "Well, hello, you."

"Hello," I replied. I wanted to grab him and smother him with kisses that would lead to other things, but I didn't know how weak he was. I didn't want to break him or anything, not now that I actually had him. "How are you feeling?"

He thought about that. It didn't take long. "Like I'd fucking kill someone for a cheeseburger."

When I laughed he added, "No, seriously. I'm ravenous. Ravenous and horny."

I was laughing, and tears were running down my cheeks. I didn't care. "Which do you want to take care of first?"

With effort, he raised his head off the pillow. He obviously was still very weak, but if the grin on his face was anything to go by, he was deliriously happy. "Well," he said, "I could eat you. Kill two birds with one stone."

I had to force my voice to remain steady. "I'd be okay with that."

AT ONE point, we fell off the bed.

In fairness, we were making up for lost time, and were experimenting a bit. We'd done fast and furious, we'd done slow and romantic and loving, and somewhere along the line, we decided to try something new and, frankly, tricky. All I knew was that, somehow, I ended up standing on the bed and Robbie was wrapped around me, and I think the idea was that we were going to use the headboard to balance us, but my foot got caught in the bed sheets, and down we went.

We ended up finishing on the floor. It was just easier that way.

Reluctantly, we untangled. Robbie was breathing hard, and beads of sweat showed on his forehead. He may have been bruised as well, but we could always pretend it was caused by the falling off the bed if any marks showed.

He pulled one of the sheets off the bed to wipe off his face. "That was… athletic."

I laughed, which made me cough. Hard. And the coughing made me laugh more. "That's one way to put it," I said as soon as words were possible.

"You okay there, old man?"

"Hey! We're the same age, give or take a few months!"

"Yeah? You wanna go out and ask someone on the street who's older?"

I rose, using the mattress for leverage. We'd been going at it hot and heavy for over an hour, and my legs weren't sure they wanted to work. I found my underwear buried among the bedsheets. They were torn. I tossed them aside. "So much for those."

"Speaking of." Robbie lay back, looking tired but happy. He yanked a pillow from off the bed to put under his head. "I need clothes. I can't keep borrowing yours."

"You can go shopping with Gina. She needs more stuff too."

"Yeah, about that. You could have told me that she was going to show up that night in a different body."

"I didn't know for sure when it would happen, and there really wasn't time for explanations once we got there."

"Still, I don't know what shocked me more, seeing Moore throttling you or some gal I didn't think I knew striding in and being all witchy."

"I was surprised, myself. I wasn't sure if she'd be able to transmogrify in time. There was always the chance that we'd have had to tackle Moore without her."

"Then we would have been fucked." Robbie sighed contentedly. "I'm hungry."

"Again? You've eaten about fifteen meals since you woke up yesterday."

"Hey, you try going that long without tasting food."

"You'll get fat."

He patted his stomach, which was admittedly tight. "Yeah. I'm worried."

I kicked him gently. He laughed and grabbed hold of my leg. I struggled, but the guy was getting a lot of his strength back, and he had one hell of a grip on my ankle. Eventually, he pulled me down to the floor, and we rolled about a little until he was lying on top of me. He kissed me gently.

"So," he said, "what now?"

"I thought we'd get some food in you and then come back for round two." I eyed the bed. "Once we get the sheets all back into place. We've made one hell of a mess."

"Fuck the bed."

I smiled. "I'd rather—"

Robbie put a finger on my lips to shut me up. "Actually, I wasn't talking about the immediate future, but long term. How do we handle this?"

"What do you mean? We celebrate! We—"

"I mean, how do I live? I'm dead. Got a grave marker and everything to prove it."

I couldn't pretend I hadn't been thinking about such things. I sighed. "Well, I can get you a new identity like I did with Gina. My contacts can hook you up with papers." I looked up at his beautiful, beautiful face and placed my hands on his cheeks. Oh, those dark eyes. If we could lie there for eternity with him on top and being able to feel his weight on me, I'd be happy. I smiled sadly. "But we do have some things to think about. Like possibly moving to another place."

"What's wrong with the apartment?"

"I meant a different city. You have family here. Your cousin Jason. Your mom and dad. What if one of them sees you? How could we explain that you're suddenly alive?"

Robbie rolled off me, and we lay there side by side, staring up at the ceiling. "You can't leave Indy. Your job is here. Gina's here. Nick's here. You can't leave your friends."

"Yes, but—"

I wasn't watching his face, but I sensed he was grinning. "I can do the Clark Kent thing. When I go out, I'll wear glasses and comb my hair so that I look like a doofus."

"That won't take much," I said. In return, Robbie punched my arm. "Ow! Holy crap, that hurt!"

"Sorry. Forgot I was human and that you could feel that."

"Yeah, I'm sure it just slipped your mind."

Robbie turned toward me. "Seriously, it's a big city. We'll figure something out." He snaked a hand over to play with my chest hair. "Ooo, there's a gray one!"

"Shut up!"

"I'll have to get a job. Wow. I hadn't thought of that. I can work again."

"Just don't think you're going to deliver pizzas again. Nothing involving driving."

"I was thinking about going to work for this guy I know. Has his own detective agency."

"Yeah? Anyone I know?"

Robbie's grin widened. "Maybe. Bastard owes me a hell of a lot of back pay. Seems that since I was dead, he didn't think he actually had to pay me."

"I don't know if I'll ever be able to pay all that back."

He slid back on top of me, and I put my arms around him. I could feel his hard-on pressing against me. "I can think of ways you can work it off."

We kissed, tenderly at first, but it soon became a fight to see whose tongue could be shoved farther into the other's mouth. When we came up for air, I said, "I thought you were hungry."

Robbie kissed me again, first on the lips, and then he shifted and kissed my chin. And then my neck. I hissed as his lips touched the soft flesh there. I always did have a tender neck. I could feel the smile on his lips as he nibbled at my skin.

"You'll leave a hickey."

"Deal with it," he muttered. He moved down my body, kissing me as he went.

Yes, the future would hold some problems for us. But at least we had each other. We'd deal with them. There wasn't a problem we couldn't solve, not now that we were together again.

I resolved not to worry about the future and concentrate on the present.

Robbie's kisses went down my abdomen and onto my crotch. I thought they might linger there, but he surprised me and shifted his body around so the kisses could continue down my leg. He scooted farther down, and when he got to my feet, lifted one and, eying me seductively as he did so, took my big toe into his mouth. He sucked at it briefly, which made me chuckle, and then released the foot. He then lifted my legs into the air.

I nearly lost my breath. "What are you doing?"

"What does it look like I'm doing?"

"Well...." I paused. "I… it's been a long time."

"No shit, Sherlock. I think I know that. Don't worry. I'll be gentle." He smiled mischievously. "As gentle as you've been with me."

I'd gone out earlier and bought the biggest tube of lubricant the corner drug store had. Now I wondered if there'd be enough. "Just… start off slow."

Robbie's eyes twinkled. "You'll love it. You're not really complaining, are you?"

I shook my head. "My days of complaining are over."

If my days of complaining hadn't been over, I might have had just one. It was over much too soon.

Luckily, we now had all our lives to experiment, to make love, to fondle, to touch, and to cherish each other.

STEPHEN OSBORNE has been an improvisational comedian, a pizza restaurant manager, and a bookseller. Other than writing, his addictions include British television shows, reading mysteries, and (a recent addition) Broadway musicals. He lives in rural Illinois with Jadzia the One-Eyed Wonder Dog.

Visit him at Facebook: http://facebook.com/stephen.osborne2 and Twitter: http://twitter.com/southbendghosts. You can contact him at leftyIN@yahoo.com.

PALE AS A
GHOST

STEPHEN OSBORNE

http://www.dreamspinnerpress.com

ANIMAL INSTINCT

STEPHEN OSBORNE

http://www.dreamspinnerpress.com

THE SCARLET TIDE

STEPHEN OSBORNE

http://www.dreamspinnerpress.com

Rat
Bastard

Stephen Osborne

http://www.dreamspinnerpress.com

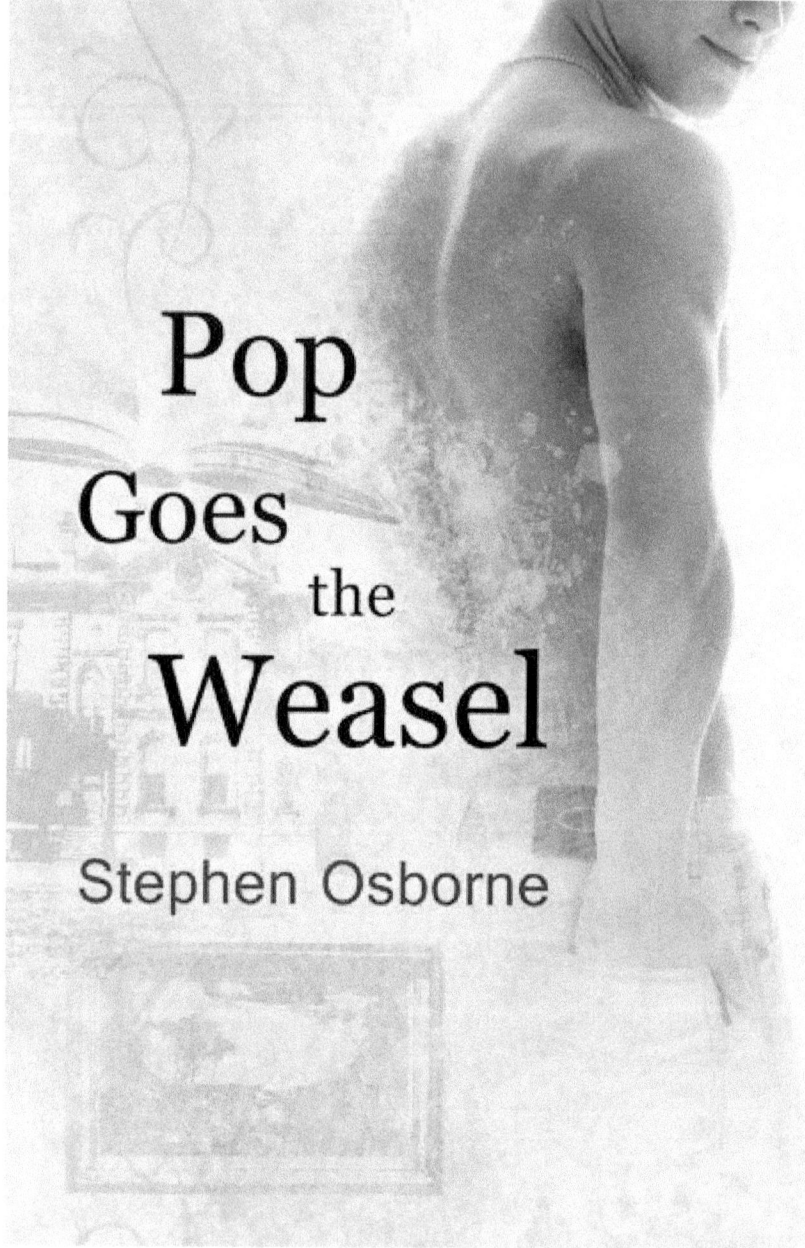

Pop
Goes
the
Weasel

Stephen Osborne

http://www.dreamspinnerpress.com

STEPHEN OSBORNE

WRESTLING WITH JESUS

http://www.dreamspinnerpress.com

FISH AND GHOSTS

RHYS FORD

http://www.dreamspinnerpress.com

DEAD MEN
Tell Tales
A NEW EDEN TALE
ANTONIO

http://www.dreamspinnerpress.com

http://www.dreamspinnerpress.com

http://www.dreamspinnerpress.com

KIM FIELDING

http://www.dreamspinnerpress.com

RIDER JACOBS

FORGOTTEN

http://www.dreamspinnerpress.com

www.ingramcontent.com/pod-product-compliance
Lightning Source LLC
Chambersburg PA
CBHW060058260626
47160CB00005B/1709